LINCOLN MIDDLE SCHO
Learning Reso...

W9-CCE-976

OTHING
TO LOSE

LINCOLN MIDDLE SCHOOL
Learning Resource Center
District #64
Park Ridge, IL 60068

WITHDRAWN

NOTHING TO LOSE

A ROBYN HUNTER MYSTERY

NORAH McCLINTOCK

LINCOLN MIDDLE SCHOOL
Learning Resource Center
District #64
Park Ridge, IL 60068

MINNEAPOLIS

First U.S. edition published in 2012 by Lerner Publishing Group, Inc.

Text copyright © 2007 by Norah McClintock. All rights reserved.
Published by arrangement with Scholastic Canada Ltd.

All U.S. rights reserved. No part of this book may be reproduced,
stored in a retrieval system, or transmitted in any form or by
any means—electronic, mechanical, photocopying, recording,
or otherwise—without the prior written permission of Lerner
Publishing Group, Inc., except for the inclusion of brief
quotations in an acknowledged review.

Darby Creek
A division of Lerner Publishing Group, Inc.
241 First Avenue North
Minneapolis, MN 55401 U.S.A.

Website address: www.lernerbooks.com

The image in this book is used with the permission of: Front and
Back Cover: © Mangojuicy/Dreamstime.com.

Main body text set in Janson Text Lt Std 11.5/15.
Typeface provided by Linotype AG.

Library of Congress Cataloging-in-Publication Data

McClintock, Norah.
    Nothing to lose / by Norah McClintock.
       p.   cm. — (Robyn Hunter mysteries ; #3)
    ISBN: 978-0-7613-8313-0 (lib. bdg. : alk. paper)
    [1. Mystery and detective stories. 2. Illegal aliens—Fiction.
   3. Human smuggling—Fiction. 4. Smuggling—Fiction.]
   I. Title.
   PZ7.M478414184No 2012
   [Fic]—dc23   2011018834

Manufactured in the United States of America
1 – SB – 12/31/11

To the bird rescuers.

CHAPTER **ONE**

"This is stupid," Morgan said. She had said the same thing when we first found ourselves in this situation two days earlier.

"It was your idea," I pointed out.

"Actually, it was *Billy's* idea."

"But you agreed to it."

No one had been more surprised than me—well, except maybe Billy—when Morgan had said, "Sure. Let's do it."

At the time I'd said, "You *do* realize that it means you'll have to get up at four in the morning?" She had given me a withering look—how dare I question her enthusiasm for all things Billy? But that was then.

"You should have stopped me," she said. "It's Saturday morning—barely. I should be in bed."

"Right," I said. I couldn't have stopped Morgan any more than I could have stopped a hurricane.

"Billy's a sweet guy," she said, "but this is crazy."

"You just figured that out?" I said.

"I'm freezing, Robyn. My fingers are numb. I'm shivering all over. I can't believe I let Billy talk me into this."

Morgan had spent a lifetime teasing Billy—for being sensitive, for being a vegan, for being an animal rights activist, for being just about everything that made Billy Billy. She had also spent the better part of a month telling me that there was no way she could ever go out with him. There was no chemistry, she said. No sparks. And then something had happened. Something that made her dewy-eyed every time Billy slipped an arm around her. Something that made her *let* Billy slip his arm around her without her threatening to send him straight to the emergency room. Something that had also made her agree to this. I still didn't understand how it had happened.

"You notice *I'm* not complaining," I said. "You notice that I didn't complain when we came down here two days ago, either." I hoped she would take the hint. I should have known better.

"I wouldn't complain, either, if I were you," she said. "By six thirty *you'll* be on your way home. You can crawl into bed and sleep until noon." Actually, she was wrong about that. But I couldn't get a word in. "*I* have to head all the way across town with Billy to band and release these things," she said. "Did I tell you that he lets me put the bands on? *Lets*. It's his idea of a treat. But guess what? It's not. You know what I've learned in the past couple of days, Robyn?" I didn't, but I was confident she was going to tell me anyway. "I've learned I don't like birds. They have beady, black, evil little eyes. And when you try to put bands on them, most of them freak out. And their toenails, or whatever you call them, can be as sharp as razors. Same goes for their beaks. I can't stand them."

A happy thought occurred to her.

"Maybe we'll get lucky today," she said. "Maybe Billy won't find any live ones."

"That's what I like about you, Morgan," I said. "You're so compassionate."

We left the shelter of the building we had been walking along and stepped out into the street, where we were hit by a gust of wind. A *north* wind. Morgan shivered and cursed.

"I need coffee *right now*," she said. "Latte. Extra large." She looked up at the black sky. "I hate this."

"Look on the bright side," I said. "You agreed to do this right at the end of fall migration season. Maybe by the time *spring* migration rolls around, you and Billy will no longer be an item."

"If I don't get some caffeine into my system, Billy and I will no longer be an item by the time sunrise rolls around."

"Hey, guys," someone called. I nudged Morgan. She turned, and we both watched as Billy's beanpole figure rounded a corner. He had a bird net tucked under one arm, a big basket slung over the other, and was carrying something in his hands.

"Is that what I think it is?" Morgan said. I wasn't sure—it was still pretty dark—but I thought I saw a tiny smile on her face.

"There's this all-night place just around the corner," Billy said. He handed Morgan a beaker-sized travel mug. "Latte," he said. "With a vanilla flavor shot."

Morgan's eyes got all big and dewy. She took the mug from Billy and went up on tiptoes to kiss him on the cheek.

"You're the best," she said, sounding sweet and girly—in other words, not at all like her normal self. But that's what love does to people, right?

Billy's grin was goofy and blissful. He handed me a smaller mug.

"Hot chocolate," he said.

"Thanks, Billy," I said. "What about you? Do you want something?" Billy won't touch any food that contains animal products. He always travels with plenty of vegan snacks because he's hungry all the time. This morning he had put his snacks in my backpack so that he could fill his backpack with the dead birds he picked up and sealed in plastic freezer bags.

"Do I have any muffins left?" he said.

"I think you ate them all on the bus," I said. I turned around so that he could unzip my backpack. "There are a couple of—"

"I see 'em," Billy said. He inspected the items in my backpack one by one and finally pulled out what he wanted—a nutrient bar that looked like shoe leather and smelled like the inside of a barn. Billy took a big bite. As he chewed, I heard a loud rustling sound. Morgan and I peeked into the basket that Billy had set down. There were three brown paper bags in it—two small, one very large. Each bag was folded over at the top and held shut with a couple of paper clips. Whatever was in the largest of the bags seemed to be trying to claw its way out. It was making a lot of noise.

"What's in there?" Morgan said. "A condor?"

"A woodcock," Billy said. Woodcocks were big birds. Some of them were even bigger than pigeons. "It was unconscious when I found it, but it sounds like it's bounced back. I think I'm going to be able to release it later." His face suddenly went slack. He started patting his pockets.

"What's the matter?" Morgan said.

"Bands," Billy said. "I think I forgot to bring the bands."

"No, you didn't," I said. "You gave them to me when you gave me your snacks. And your bird book. And the tagging kit. And all the rest of your supplies." Billy's stuff was really weighing me down.

Billy calmed down and continued to munch on his nutrient bar.

"I also found a couple of hermit thrushes," he said between bites. "I'm not sure if they're going to make it, though. One of them looks like it's in bad shape. I'm gonna have to take it in and have it checked over."

Good old Billy. There wasn't anything he wouldn't do to help the creatures of the earth, even if it meant getting up in the middle of the night to rescue birds in the office-tower jungle of the financial district. And recruiting volunteers, like us, to help him. Last year Billy and a university professor he had met at an animal rights get-together had founded DARC—the Downtown Avian Rescue Club.

DARC is the medical corps in the war between migrating birds and downtown office buildings. Migration season runs from mid-March to early June and again from mid-August to mid-November. I learned from Billy that most small birds migrate at night. These birds are attracted to lights—lights left on in office towers, lights on high monuments, lights in lighthouses, and lights on bridges. Sometimes when migrating birds crash into these brightly lit office towers or bridges, they die on impact. Billy calls these primary kills.

But sometimes they survive. Sometimes when they hit a building or a monument or a bridge, they're only dazed. Then they fall—ten stories, twenty stories, more—down to the concrete below. Sometimes it's the fall that kills them. Sometimes it's the shock or trauma or exposure after they hit the ground that kills them. Or sometimes predators—cats, rats, raccoons—find them dazed or hurt, and they pounce. Billy calls these secondary kills.

That's why we were downtown in the extremely early hours of the morning. We were trying to prevent secondary kills by picking up as many live birds as we could find. If they were hurt, we took them to an animal shelter for medical attention. If they were just dazed, we tucked them into brown paper bags and gave them time to recover before releasing them in a nearby park. We also picked up all the dead birds we found—well, Billy picked them up.

A few days earlier, he had opened a freezer in the DARC office to show us all the birds he had collected so far this season. The small freezer was filled with plastic baggies, each one containing a dead bird and bearing a label that recorded the species, the date it had been found, and where it had been picked up. Morgan's reaction: "*Eeew!*" Mine? Okay, initially I had also thought *eeew*. But then I had taken a second look and noticed how small the birds were. One of them was no bigger than my thumb.

"That's a hummingbird," Billy had said.

Even Morgan looked again. "It's so tiny." She edged closer to the freezer.

"That's a warbler," Billy said. "And that's a song sparrow. And an ovenbird. And a kinglet. . . ."

Morgan's expression had changed slowly from revulsion to admiration. Maybe she didn't care much about birds, but even she couldn't help being impressed by Billy's knowledge.

"What about the dead ones?" I said now, between sips of hot chocolate.

Billy's expression grew grim.

"I've got seventeen so far," he said. I glanced at his backpack. It was the same one he wore to school most days. "Why don't you two take a break and warm up?" he said. "I'm going to do another walk around that building." He nodded at the tallest office tower in the financial district. It was lit up like a Christmas tree, even though there were probably only a few security guards inside.

Morgan sipped her latte while Billy disappeared around a corner. I thought she would want to take shelter somewhere, but instead she turned to me and said, "Why don't we check out that building over there?"

She pointed to the second-tallest office tower, which was lit up like a slightly smaller Christmas tree. With our hot beverages in one hand, our bird nets in the other, and our backpacks on our backs, we set off across the street. As we patrolled one side of the building, we saw what looked like a heap of old blankets inside a bus shelter. Morgan shook her head.

"Pretty strange, huh?" she said.

"What?"

"We're down here in the middle of the night rescuing birds."

"Yeah. And?"

"And all around us there are homeless people sleeping outside in the cold because they have no place to go. You don't think that's weird?"

I looked more closely at the heap of blankets in the bus shelter and saw that it had a head. We had also seen two homeless men scrunched up in sleeping bags on the sidewalk when we'd first gotten off the bus.

"Did you know that Billy volunteers at a homeless shelter once a week?" Morgan said.

Of course I knew. Unlike Morgan, I usually paid attention when Billy talked. After all, he was my friend.

"He's such a good guy," Morgan said.

I knew that too.

"I've known him since—what?—second grade," she said. "How'd it take me so long to realize what a great guy he is?" And there she was, going dewy-eyed again. "I think maybe next time he goes to the shelter, I'll go with him."

It was hard to believe, but Morgan was perilously close to becoming a caring person.

"Uh-oh," she said.

"What?"

She pointed. "Uh-oh" was right. I counted three small, motionless bodies, and Billy was nowhere in sight. We looked at each other, and Morgan made a face. With a sigh, I gave her my hot chocolate, shrugged off my backpack, and took out some plastic bags and gloves. One by icky one, I picked up three dead birds and sealed the bags. I held them out to Morgan.

"No way," she said.

I put the dead birds in their plastic bags into another plastic bag. I put that bag into a paper bag meant to hold live birds. I didn't want those birds to touch any of my things. Reluctantly, I dropped the paper bag into my backpack. *Note to self*, I thought, *disinfect backpack before using it again*. I was slipping my backpack on again—and trying hard not to think about the small bodies inside it—when Morgan said, "I hate to tell you this, but I think I see another one." She pointed to a small dark spot on the concrete up ahead.

"If it's a bird, it's yours," I said.

"Hey!" Morgan grabbed my arm. "Look."

A large bird—even I recognized it as a seagull—was hovering far above the street. It tucked itself in and began a tight, swift dive.

"Didn't Billy say—"

"Yep."

Billy had said that along with cats and rats and raccoons, seagulls also prey on wounded songbirds. So when I saw the gull aim itself at that small dark spot on the concrete—a dark spot that I saw was fluttering weakly—I dropped my backpack and took off down the sidewalk. I raised my net while I ran and started to lower it as I got close to the dark spot.

Unfortunately, the seagull reached the spot before I did and opened its beak to snatch the tiny, helpless creature.

"Hey!" I shouted. I thought if I yelled loud enough, it would startle the gull off. I should have known better. The pigeons in this city are so indifferent to people that you have to walk around them. Why should the seagulls be any different? I shouted again, louder this time. The gull didn't even turn to look at me. I didn't know what else to do, so I poked it with my bird net. What do you know? It worked. The gull launched itself back into the air.

I looked down at the pavement where I had first spotted the little bird. It was gone. I looked up at the gull. Had it scooped up the dazed, wounded bird without me noticing? I didn't see anything in the gull's beak. And the gull, which had retreated to a safe height, was tucking itself up again to prepare for another dive.

I scouted the pavement frantically for the little bird and found it cowering next to the base of the office tower. The gull must have spotted it too, because it was diving directly at that spot.

I thought, *No problem. I'm a lot bigger than a seagull. I'll protect the little bird by positioning myself between it and the gull. I'll put my net over it so that it can't skitter away and the gull can't grab it.*

It seemed like a good plan, but (a) I didn't know much about seagulls in general, and (b) I didn't know anything about this seagull in particular.

It turned out to be the Terminator of the seagull world. Nothing—and no one—was going to stop it from getting what it wanted, especially not a mere human like me.

One minute my feet were firmly planted, my arms were flapping, and I was yelling, "Shoo, shoo, shoo!" The next minute—the minute I realized that this gull was prepared to go through me if it couldn't get around me—I was cowering, shielding my head, and screaming as it flew right at me.

I must have looked at Morgan because I have a clear memory of seeing surprise and then horror on her face.

I know I saw her drop my cup of hot chocolate and her bird net. Then I saw her turn, still holding her extra-large latte, and run away. Thanks a bunch.

With my free hand, I swung at the seagull with the long handle of my bird net. Here's something you might not know: seagulls are exceptionally sturdy birds. When I swiped at that gull—and, bird lovers, I swear it was self-defense—I was astonished at how solid its body was. On first whack, nothing happened. Then it dropped to the ground and lay motionless on the pavement.

My first thought: *Way to go, Robyn. You dragged yourself out of bed before the crack of dawn to rescue birds and what do you do? You club one to death.*

My second thought: *This seagull really* is *the Terminator.* Because just as I breathed a sigh of relief (sorry again, bird lovers), lowered my net, and turned toward the little bird, I saw movement out of the corner of my eye. The gull was stirring. Its broad wings fluttered and it righted itself. I looked back at the little bird trembling on the concrete beside me. It had fluffed out all of its feathers, maybe because it was cold or maybe because it was trying to look bigger than it actually was to scare off predators like the gull and (as far as the little bird was concerned) me. I raised my net slowly and lowered it quickly over the tiny creature. *Easy*, I thought.

Then something struck me on the shoulder. The gull squalled around me, flapping its wings and screeching. You don't realize just how big and hard and sharp-looking a gull's beak is until it's right in your face. And do you know what's at the end of those big seagull feet? Big, sharp seagull toenails. And they were right in my face.

I threw my hands up to protect myself. My net was still lying on the ground, the mesh part of it covering the little bird, which sat perfectly still. Maybe it was frozen in terror. Or maybe it felt safe under the net—I don't know. I looked down at the little creature that I was supposed to be saving and then up at the larger, screeching creature that was preventing me from carrying out my mission, and I got angry.

Very angry.

I flailed at the gull with both arms and screeched back at it: "Shoo, shoo!"

Then I heard a screech behind me: "Grah, grah!" I turned and saw Billy coming toward me at a dead run, waving his net. Morgan chugged after him, still clutching her extra-large latte. She hadn't deserted me after all. She had gone for reinforcements.

"Grah! Grah!" Billy shouted again. I followed his lead. We were two supposedly sane people, dancing in the early morning darkness, shouting ourselves hoarse until the seagull finally gave up and wheeled away.

"Thanks, Billy," I said.

"Gulls can be pretty aggressive," he said. "I read about a seagull in Britain that killed a dog. And there was another story about a woman who had to go to the hospital because a gull attacked her and its beak was embedded in her skull."

I thought he was kidding, but he looked completely serious.

"One time," he said, "I saw a gull walking down the sidewalk—*walking*—doing exactly what we do when we come out here. It was looking at the bottoms of buildings for dazed or hurt birds. Some of those gulls are pretty smart."

"Well, that gull was going after this little guy." I pointed at the dazed bird beneath my net.

Billy called to Morgan and asked if she had any paper bags in her backpack.

She handed one to him and they crouched down together on the cold concrete. I stepped aside and let them worry about transferring the little bird from my net to the brown paper bag. They made a pretty good team: calm and competent Doctor Billy and his faithful, if squeamish, assistant Morgan. While they worked, I looked around to make sure that the gull was gone for good.

That's when I saw someone dash around the far corner of the office tower, carrying *my* backpack.

CHAPTER **TWO**

I pounded down the pavement after the thief, yelling, "Hey! Hey!"

The person with my backpack glanced over his shoulder at me. He had a hat jammed down over his head and a scarf pulled up over the lower part of his face. His dirty jeans flapped around his scrawny legs as he ran. His thin jacket looked more suited to a sunny spring afternoon than to a cold November morning. When he looked back at me, his eyes were big, and for a moment, I even thought he *was* going to stop. But instead he poured on the speed.

"Hey!" I shouted again. "That's mine!"

A homeless man curled up in a sleeping bag over a subway grate raised his head, looked around, and then lowered his head again, uninterested in my personal drama.

The thief rounded a corner up ahead. I raced after him, determined to reclaim my backpack. It held my wallet, with all of my ID and money, my extra sweater (handmade, robin's-egg blue—get it?—brought back from England for me by my mother), and a whole lot of Billy's stuff. Oh, and three dead birds.

I rounded the corner a few seconds after the thief and found the streets completely deserted. No cars. No buses. No pedestrians. And no thief.

When I rejoined Billy and Morgan and breathlessly told them what had happened, Billy's expression was more stricken than mine had probably been.

"Tell me they didn't take *everything*," he said.

"He stole my backpack, Billy," I said, as patiently as I could. "He didn't empty it first."

"You mean he got all the banding equipment?" he said, as if this were the most precious thing I had been carrying.

I nodded.

Morgan positively beamed.

． ． ．

Morgan was wrong when she said I could go home and sleep until noon. I had plans. Plans that I had made the night before while my mother dashed from the basement washing machine to her bedroom on the second floor, where she was packing for a business trip.

My mother is a lawyer. She had been invited to speak at a national conference on youth and crime. For a lawyer, being invited to speak at a national conference is a *very big deal*, especially if it's your first invitation and if you want to make a good impression. Being a Type-A perfectionist, she hadn't merely prepared, she had *over*-prepared. But, as of last night, she was still convinced that she wasn't ready. She was also convinced that she hadn't packed the exact right clothes to (a) deliver her presentation, (b) be seen at the rest of the two-day conference, and (c) represent her law firm at the formal dinner that was scheduled to close the conference on Monday night. But that's my mom for you. She's good—actually, excellent—at what she does, but she always thinks she could be doing more—a *lot* more.

She was on her way upstairs with an armful of clean clothes and a small suitcase when the phone rang.

"I'll get it," I said.

She hovered on the stairs until I told her it was for me. I waited until she had scurried up to her room before I said, "Hi, Nick." My greeting came out sounding less than welcoming.

"You're mad at me," Nick said. "I can tell. Sorry, Robyn. I kept meaning to call, but I've been—" I heard a sigh on the other end of the phone. "I was going to say that I've been busy, but that's no excuse. I should have called sooner. I'm sorry, okay? *Really* sorry."

The words came out in a rush, as if he were trying to tell me everything before I hung up on him.

"What do you say, Robyn? Do you forgive me?"

"I've been calling you," I said. I'd called him every day for the past week. "But I can never get ahold of you.

You're never home. You don't have a cell phone. You don't even have an answering machine."

"I can't afford stuff like that," he said. He sounded hurt. Worse, he sounded ashamed. It bothered him sometimes—actually, a *lot* of the time—that I had the latest of almost everything while he had to scramble for the basics. He thought I cared about stuff like that. I don't.

"All I meant was . . ." What *did* I mean? "You never call me, Nick. I was beginning to think maybe you'd found someone else."

"Someone else?" he said. He sounded surprised, and that made me feel a little better. "No way, Robyn. It's just that with school and my job, some days I come home, collapse on the couch, fall asleep, and wake up with just enough time to do my homework and get to school. You know what? I have a whole lot more respect now for people who work fast food. You can't believe the kind of people you have to put up with. And you can't yell at them because they're customers and the customer—"

"—is always right. I know," I said. "So, how are you, anyway?"

"Tired."

I was glad we were talking on the phone instead of in person. It meant I didn't have to try to hide the disappointed look on my face.

"Me too," I said. "And I have to be up and out of here in a few hours."

"A few hours? Robyn, it's nearly eleven o'clock."

"I know. I have to be out of here by four thirty."

"In the *morning?*"

"Yeah."

There was a long pause on the other end of the phone before he said, "Does that mean you're going somewhere for the weekend?"

"It means I'm going somewhere for a couple of hours," I said. I filled him in on my plans and smiled at the relief in his voice. Maybe he hadn't been great at staying in touch lately, but he obviously cared about what I was up to.

"Barry finally gave me a weekend off," he said. Barry Osler was a shift manager at the restaurant where Nick worked. He was also a senior at my school. His father owned a dozen restaurants in one of the biggest fast-food chains on the planet. Barry was aiming to outdo his father. He boasted that he'd be a fast-food king himself by the time he turned thirty. He'd also asked me out a few times. I made up excuses every time. I hadn't mentioned to Nick that I knew Barry—he'd been glad when he finally landed a job and I wasn't sure how he'd feel about working for someone who asked me out now and then. I hadn't mentioned Nick to Barry, either, for more or less the same reason.

"So how about it, Robyn?" Nick said. "Why don't you meet me first thing tomorrow morning? We can spend the day together—celebrate."

"Celebrate?"

I heard a sigh of disappointment on the other end of the phone.

"I guess that means *I'm* the sentimental one in this relationship," he said. Relationship? I liked the sound of that. "Check your calendar, Robyn. I met you exactly three months ago today. At the animal shelter."

This past summer we had both volunteered—well, *sort of* volunteered—at an animal shelter. Nick had been there as part of a court-mandated anger management program. I had been there to placate a storeowner who wanted to press charges against me as a result of an incident during an animal rights demonstration. But that wasn't the first time I had laid eyes on him.

"We *met* in middle school," I said. "Remember?"

"That doesn't count."

"Why not?"

"Because back then I wasn't smart enough to appreciate you."

"*Appreciate* me?"

"Yeah. Back then I thought you were a pain. Now . . . well, you know how I feel now, Robyn. So will you meet me?"

I forgot all about being angry with him.

"Yes," I said. I told him that I would be at my father's place after I finished with Morgan and Billy. "Meet you there."

My mother was standing on the stairs frowning when I hung up the phone.

"Was that Nick?" she said. "Are you planning to see him this weekend?"

Her frown deepened when I answered yes to both questions.

"Is that a problem?" I said.

"You haven't mentioned him in a while. I thought perhaps you two had stopped seeing each other."

Knowing my mother, she had probably been *hoping* that we'd stopped seeing each other, which is why I hardly ever discussed Nick with her. My mother represented a lot of young offenders. She had even represented Nick. Most people might assume that this would make her sympathetic to their situation. And maybe it did when it came to doing her best for them in court. But she also knew the kind of trouble they could get into, and that made her want to protect me—*over*protect me—from them.

"I'm sorry, Robyn," she said. "But kids like Nick have so many issues to deal with." In other words, they weren't ideal boyfriend material.

"He's been busy. I haven't seen him in a while. But we're going to spend the day together tomorrow."

My mother did not look happy. "People have to have something in common if they're going to build a relationship, Robyn," she said. "But you and Nick . . . I know you think he's cool—"

"*Cool?*"

"You know what I mean. He's different. He's a good-looking boy with the kind of . . . past that so many girls seem to find romantic. But—"

"Mom, I like him because I like him, not because I have a thing for bad boys. Besides, he's not what you think. He's been working full-time for over a month now—*while* he's going to school. *And* we have a lot in common."

My mother shook her head. "I know I can't tell you what to do, Robyn," she said. Not that that stopped her from trying. "But when I feel strongly about something, I feel it's my responsibility as your mother to tell you. It's up to you to decide whether or not you agree."

Well, I had decided. I had made plans to spend Saturday with Nick, and I was going to keep them.

. . .

When I got home after leaving Morgan and Billy and the birds downtown, my mother was pacing in the front hall.

"I was worried," she said. "I got up and you were gone."

"I left you a note," I said.

"I know. That's why I was worried. I thought we agreed you weren't going down there again."

"*You* agreed I wasn't going," I said. "*I* disagreed. Remember?" That's why I had left her a note instead of telling her face-to-face. I didn't want to have to argue about it—again. "Mom, I'm sixteen. Besides, there was nothing to worry about. Here I am, safe and sound." I didn't mention that my backpack hadn't made the return trip with me. I hoped she wouldn't notice. If she did, she would pester me until I told her what had happened. And if I told her, she would drive me crazy until I promised never to participate in DARC activities again.

"Where exactly did you go?"

"Just downtown. We check all the office towers. Billy has been doing it for over a year, and nothing has ever happened."

"It's deserted downtown at five in the morning," my mother said. "What if anything had happened? There'd be no one around to help you."

"I wasn't alone, Mom. I was with Billy and Morgan. And there were a couple of other DARC people around. We kept running into them. We keep an eye out for each other."

My mother did not look convinced. She opened her mouth to say something else. I decided to take evasive action. I glanced at my watch and said, "Wow, it's later than I thought. Are you going to have enough time to drop me at Dad's and still get to the airport on time?"

She checked her own watch. A look of horror appeared on her face. For the next fifteen minutes she flew around the house, double-checking the contents of her big suitcase, her little suitcase, and her briefcase, triple-checking that all the windows and doors were secured, and quizzing me about whether *I* had packed everything I needed.

"Mom, I've been packing for weekends at Dad's for four years now." My parents had been separated for three years and divorced for almost exactly one year. "Besides, I have a key." Fortunately, my keys had been in my pocket, not in my backpack. "If I forget anything, I can come back and get it."

"Don't forget that you have a history essay due on Wednesday."

"It's due *next* Wednesday," I said. I grabbed my overnight bag.

"You're not taking your backpack?"

"I prefer to travel light."

She gave me a funny look. I was afraid she was going to start quizzing me about it, so I said, "Don't you have to get to the airport extra early so you can clear security?" That switched her focus again. It wasn't long before she was dropping me off on the street where my father lives. Her final words were "Be good."

CHAPTER **THREE**

As I walked toward my father's building, I thought, *Something is different. But what?* I looked up and down the block in the morning quiet, trying to figure out what it was. But I couldn't. I continued on until I got to the converted carpet factory where my father lives. When he inherited the place, it was located in a rundown part of town. But things have changed since then. These days, the area is (mostly) trendy. A lot of what used to be down-and-out apartments have been renovated and are owned by doctors, lawyers, and engineers. My father's building has been transformed too. The ground floor houses a gourmet restaurant called La Folie. The second floor consists of six apartments. My father occupies the entire, enormous third floor.

"*Hello!*" I called from the door to my father's loft.

A moment later my father shuffled out of his bedroom wearing a T-shirt and pajama bottoms. His hair was sticking out in a dozen different directions.

"Late night, Dad?" I said.

"Nearly dawn by the time I got to bed." He yawned. "Correct me if I'm wrong, but aren't you early?"

"You know Mom. She was paranoid she was going to miss her flight."

My father grinned. "Why be merely on time when you can be an hour early, just in case?" He padded by me in bare feet, heading for the kitchen. I took a seat on a stool at the counter that divided the cooking area of the kitchen from the eating area. I watched him fiddle with his coffeemaker.

"How about breakfast? You hungry, Robbie?" he said. Robbie is my father's nickname for me. It irritates my mother, who is opposed to nicknames on principle. "If I had wanted to call her Robbie," she always tells my father, "I would have named her Robbie."

"I'm okay, Dad. Besides, Nick will be here any minute."

"Knowing Nick, he'll arrive with an appetite," my father said. He poured himself a cup of coffee and asked if I wanted one. I said yes. If I was going to spend the day with Nick, I wanted to be wide awake. My father poured me a cup, and then he flipped on the radio to catch the news. He pottered around the kitchen, making plenty of noise during the political news stories. But, as usual, he stopped what he was doing when a crime-related story came on. Once a cop . . . I got busy rummaging through his fridge for some milk.

"I knew it," my father said.

"Knew what?" *A-ha!* There was the milk, way in the back behind a jar of pickles.

"There was a murder in Chinatown the other day."

Morgan and Billy and I had been right near Chinatown, but I hadn't told my mother. She, like my father, followed the crime news. My father did it because he couldn't help himself. My mother did it because she was a concerned citizen and worried parent. If she knew I had been mere blocks away from where a shooting had taken place—especially in the pitch black with hardly anyone around—she would have freaked out for sure.

"At first, the police couldn't identify the victim," my father said. "Now they're saying he was in the country illegally. Apparently he's from the same part of China as those people they found in that shipping container. You heard about that, Robbie?"

I nodded. Nineteen dead bodies had been discovered in a shipping container down by the docks. It had made the front page of every newspaper in town.

"The man who was shot had been in the country longer. It looks like a human-trafficking ring is responsible—just as I suspected."

"Good for you, Dad," I said as I pulled out the carton of milk and reluctantly took a sniff. Fresh as a baby's breath. Victory!

"It's appalling," my father said, undeterred by my lack of interest. "There may have been close to fifty people in that shipping container. Nineteen of them dead from illness and dehydration. Can you imagine? And the ones who made it here alive aren't out of the woods yet. They'll be exploited till they can pay off what they owe."

I poured some milk into my coffee and took a sip. Perfect. "I read about it in the paper, Dad," I said. "They think the people were locked in there for over a month." I shuddered as I thought about it—people locked up like prisoners for a month-long voyage in a container intended to hold cargo, not human beings. They had eaten in there, slept in there, done everything else in there—and, according to the news, the survivors had spent at least some of their time locked in with dead people. "Why would anyone agree to conditions like that? Why would they take the chance?"

"We have it pretty good here," my father said. "But a lot of people aren't so fortunate. A lot are downright desperate—so desperate that they'll do anything for a chance to better their lives. Anytime there are people who are that desperate, there are always other people who find a way to profit—who'll bring people into a country illegally, for a price. Happens all over the world. The Mexican-American border is a human-smuggling hotspot. People pay smugglers to get them across the border. In Mexico they call the smugglers coyotes. In China they're called snakeheads."

"Snakeheads?"

He nodded. "They're criminals," he said. "But in some places, the big snakeheads—the ones who finance the whole undertaking by providing a ship, for example—those guys are often so-called legitimate businessmen. They invest in trafficking the same way they invest in legal business opportunities. Of course, they always make sure that nothing can be traced back to them. Most of them have some kind of link to one or other of the triads—Chinese gangs. They're into all kinds of criminal activities."

"Including smuggling people."

"Exactly. The past few years, there have been reports of groups of Chinese immigrants being smuggled into a lot of different countries. Australia, across Europe, Canada, the U.S. They pay big money to be smuggled in. For a price, the smugglers also forge identity papers—visas and passports." He took a sip of coffee. "Smuggling is one thing—people pay smugglers to help them get around the law. But human trafficking? That's even worse."

"There's a difference?"

"Smuggling and trafficking are similar, except trafficking involves exploitation—coercion. Say the people who want to be smuggled in don't have enough money to pay the snakeheads. The snakeheads'll offer to lend them the money and tell them that they can pay it back after they reach their destination. Once the immigrants get where they're going, the snakeheads force them to work long hours in illegal sweatshops to pay off their debt. Sometimes they force them to get involved in activities like the drug trade. The immigrants can't do anything about it—they're in the country illegally. They complain, they're deported. Sometimes the traffickers threaten to kill them if they don't cooperate. Or they threaten their families back home."

"Why would anyone agree to that?" I said.

"Like I said, we have it pretty good here, Robbie. And the snakeheads don't always tell the immigrants what they're in for."

"But the people who pay the smugglers must know that they have a chance of getting caught and sent back."

My father shrugged. "Sometimes they believe rumors circulated by the snakeheads, like the ones about amnesties."

"Amnesties?"

"A few years back, a rumor went around that there was going to be a general amnesty for all illegal immigrants, to mark the new millennium. Wasn't true. But it encouraged a lot of people to book passage with snakeheads. There are always a lot of rumors about kids, that children have a better chance of being allowed to stay if they're caught by Immigration. As to the conditions . . ." He shrugged again. "I used to know a guy"—knowing my father, he meant a cop—"who did liaison work with the immigration department. He told me that one Chinese man who got caught said that the snakeheads told him that he would arrive here on a luxury ship. A movie theater on board, good food. It was an out-and-out lie. But by the time the guy found out, it was too late to do anything about it."

"The man who was shot—do they think he was a snakehead?"

"That I don't know." My father snapped off the radio. "I'm making eggs," he said. "Sure I can't interest you?"

"I'm going to wait and see what Nick wants to do," I said. I glanced at my watch again. "He said he would pick me up early. He has plans for us."

"Suit yourself," my father said. "I'm making them scrambled . . ."

My mouth started to water. My father made excellent scrambled eggs. His secret ingredients were a touch of cream cheese and some fresh chives.

"I'll wait," I said.

My father shrugged and opened the fridge.

"Dad?"

I think it was the hesitation in my voice that made his ex-cop radar blip. When his head emerged from the fridge, he was on full alert.

"I was robbed this morning," I said.

"What do you mean, robbed? Where? Did someone break into the house?"

"I was downtown with Billy and Morgan. Someone stole my backpack."

He shut the fridge door without taking out any eggs. "Were you hurt?"

I shook my head. "I wasn't wearing my backpack at the time." I explained what had happened. "There wasn't a lot of money in my wallet," I said. "But I had my bus pass in it, my student ID. Some pictures." Snapshots of Nick and Orion, the dog he walked regularly, and one of Nick with his arm around me.

"Cell phone?" he said.

"No." That had been in my jacket pocket. I had lost my last phone a while back and my father had replaced it for me.

"You didn't have your credit cards in your wallet, did you, Robbie?"

I shook my head.

"Dad, I don't have any credit cards."

"Did you report the loss to the police?"

"I didn't even report it to Mom," I said. My father nodded. He knew what would have happened if I'd told my mother.

"I'll call someone," he said. "I don't know if you'll get your stuff back, Robbie, but you never know. If there have been other similar thefts in the area, maybe they'll catch the guy." He poured himself another cup of coffee before picking up the phone and calling the police.

"Someone will be here in a few minutes," he said when he hung up.

"A few *minutes?*" I said. That was fast. "Lemme guess—a friend of yours?"

My father grinned. He knew a lot of people and made a point of keeping in touch. "It's not what you know," he said, over and over. "It's who you know and what *they* know." He believed that in his line of work— private security and investigations—you were only as good as your contacts.

While we waited, my father cracked some eggs into a frying pan and put some bread in the toaster. While he stirred the eggs, he said, "So, has your mother made up her mind yet about what's-his-name?" He tried to sound casual, as if no matter what the answer was, it was no big deal. Maybe he really thought that. Maybe.

"His name is Ted Gold," I said, even though my father knew it perfectly well. Ted had asked my mother to marry him. She hadn't said yes yet, but she hadn't said no, either. "And you know I'm not supposed to talk about him." My mother had forbidden me to discuss any aspect of her private life with my father.

"Well, what do *you* think, Robbie? Do you think she's going to marry him?"

I shrugged. I really had no idea. I knew that my mother liked Ted—a lot. But I also knew that she didn't seem in any hurry to remarry.

Someone knocked on the door. It couldn't have been my father's police officer friend—he would have to be buzzed up through the ground-floor security door. That meant it had to be Nick, who lived directly below my father.

I was right. Nick came in, glanced around—checking, I think, to see where my father was. When he didn't see him, he pulled me close and kissed me. "I missed you," he said in a low voice.

"I missed you too." I wrapped my arms around his waist, and we just stood there for a moment, my head resting against his chest so that I heard his heart beating, until I heard a noise behind me—my father, clearing his throat. I pulled away from Nick.

"I was just about to have breakfast, Nick," my father said. "Can I get you something?"

"Uh, no, thanks," Nick said. But I could tell he was torn. My father was probably right. Nick was probably hungry. "Robyn and I have plans. We'll grab something downtown."

My father sat down with his eggs and toast and a fresh cup of coffee. On the surface he looked friendly and relaxed. But I knew him better than most people, which is why I knew that he was doing what he always did: examining, assessing, analyzing. "So how's everything going, Nick?" he said.

"Good," Nick said.

My father looked him over carefully. Nick looked pretty much the same as he always did. He was wearing black boots, a black hoodie, and black jeans. His jet-black hair, which was getting long, was tucked back behind his ears. A lock of it fell over his purple-blue eyes. A hairline scar ran from the bridge of his nose clear across to his right earlobe. Nick smiled pleasantly at my father but raised a hand to adjust his collar. That's when I noticed the mark on his neck. It was an ugly black-and-purple bruise. I caught a glimpse of it just before he hid it under his hood. I was sure my father had also noticed, but he didn't mention it. Instead, he doubled down on his eggs.

"We should get going," Nick said.

I was about to explain that I had to wait for my father's police officer friend when the buzzer sounded. That's when it hit me.

"The dog," I said.

"Huh?" Nick said.

"See who it is, will you, Robbie?" my father said, his mouth full of eggs.

I pushed the button on the wall next to the intercom and said hello.

"Stan Rogers here to see Mac Hunter," a voice said.

"Buzz him in, Robbie," my father said.

I buzzed the visitor through. While I waited for him to reach the top of the stairs, I turned back to Nick. "There's a dog that lives somewhere around here," I said. "It must practically live outside. It barks every time someone gets close to this building. You can always tell when someone is coming. You haven't heard it?"

Nick just shrugged.

"The thing is," I said, "I didn't hear it this morning. I knew something was different, but I couldn't figure out what. Maybe they took the poor thing inside for a change." Then another thought struck me. "I hope it didn't die or anything."

I heard footsteps out in the hall and opened the door. Stan Rogers turned out to be a uniformed police officer, which didn't surprise me. What *did* surprise me, though, was the look on Nick's face when I ushered Stan in. His smile vanished. He stared at Stan Rogers as if he were facing down an old enemy. *Uh-oh*, I thought.

CHAPTER **FOUR**

My father crossed over to the door and clasped Stan Rogers by the hand. The two of them stood in the doorway for a few moments, catching up. When my father finally got around to introducing me, Stan beamed.

"You probably don't remember," he said, "but you sat on my knee, oh, a dozen or so years ago."

"Stan used to play Santa Claus at the Christmas parties we had at the division where I worked when you were little," my father said.

Stan was middle-aged and a little on the plump side. He had clear blue eyes that twinkled when he smiled. I bet he made a terrific Santa.

"I'm still on Santa detail," he said. "Scheduled to suit up again in a couple of weeks. I can't believe that Christmas is only six weeks away. Where does the time go, huh?" He glanced across the room at Nick.

My father followed his gaze. "Nick D'Angelo," he said. "Nick is a friend of Robbie's."

Stan nodded stiffly before turning back to me. "So, I understand you want to report a theft."

"That's right," my father said. "Have a seat, Stan." He gestured to an empty chair. "I'll get you some coffee while you take Robbie's information."

Stan sat down, pulled out a notebook, and started to write down all the details of what he called "the incident"—the street where it had happened, when it had happened, the building I had been standing in front of, the make of my backpack, and a description of the thief. He also wrote down everything that had been in the backpack, like my sweater. "A really pretty robin's-egg blue color," I told him. "Handmade, not machine-made."

"Anything else?" he said.

"Three dead birds."

"Oh?" He waited patiently for an explanation, so I told him about DARC and what I had been doing downtown.

"There was also some DARC stuff in my backpack," I said. This was an official police report, so I figured I should be thorough. "The only thing that's really valuable is the banding equipment."

"Banding equipment?"

Stan, my father, and Nick were all looking at me, curious.

"There's a professor at the university who works with DARC," I said. "He's studying a certain kind of thrush. Whenever Billy or anyone else finds one of these thrushes and it's in good enough shape to be released, it gets banded. The band is a little radio transmitter, so the professor can track them. I think there were half a dozen of them in my backpack."

"You had six radio transmitters in there?" Stan said. He glanced over my shoulder to where my father was standing. I knew exactly what he was thinking.

"You have to activate them before they start sending out a signal," I said. "And they weren't activated."

Stan shook his head. "Too bad. Do you think you would recognize the thief again if you saw him?"

I said I wasn't sure. The thief had been wearing a hat pulled down low over his forehead and a scarf pulled up high over his chin and mouth. The only part of his face that I had really got a good look at—and only for a second or two—was his eyes. Stan closed his notebook.

"I can't make any promises," he said. "But you never know." He stood up and tucked his notebook into a pocket. He glanced at Nick again but didn't say anything. "I'll be in touch if anything comes up."

My father thanked Stan for coming and showed him to the door. They stood out in the hall for a few minutes. I heard them talking in low voices. When my father came back inside, he looked at Nick. His eyes lingered on Nick's turned-up collar. Nick started to squirm. Then the phone rang. My father answered it, carried the phone into his office, and shut the door. I turned to Nick.

"You know that cop, don't you?" I said.

"I've seen him around."

What did that mean? "Is he a friend of Glen's?"

Glen Ross was Nick's aunt's boyfriend. He was also the reason that Nick was living on his own instead of with his aunt. The last time Glen and Nick had had an argument, Nick had ended up with a sprained wrist.

Nick didn't answer.

"Did you have another argument with Glen?"

"I haven't seen him in over a week," he said. From his bitter tone, I guessed that he hadn't seen his aunt either.

"So how did you get that bruise on your neck?"

"What bruise?"

"Wrong answer, Nick." I reached out and pulled down his collar.

"Oh, that," he said. "I had a difference of opinion with someone else. It's no big deal." He slipped an arm around my waist and held me close. I knew he was only doing it to stop me from asking more questions, but I have to admit, it felt good.

"It could be a big deal if the other person got hurt and decides to press charges," I said. I felt him tense up against me. "I don't want you to end up in trouble again."

"Neither do I," he said. "Especially now." Now that he was sixteen, he meant, when the courts could go harder on him if the trouble was serious enough. He held me tighter, then suddenly let go and stepped back. I didn't need eyes in the back of my head to know that my father had emerged from his office.

"So, what are you two up to this weekend?" he said.

Nick just shrugged. What was wrong with him? He and my dad usually got along great. Nick even told me once that he admired my father. But today he was closed up tighter than a bank after business hours.

"Nick has the weekend off for a change," I said. "We're going to spend some time together." I grabbed my jacket off the chair where I had dropped it when I arrived.

"I need a word with you before you go, Robbie."

I looked at him expectantly.

"In private," he said.

Nick shifted uncomfortably and stared at the floor.

"Excuse us for a minute, Nick," my father said. I followed him into his office. It was one of the few "rooms" in the place that had a door, but my father left it open. "That phone call I just got—it was business. I have to go out of town."

"No problem."

"I probably won't be back tonight. I want you to stay with Henri."

Henri is Henrietta Saint-Onge, girlfriend of my father's business partner Vernon Deloitte, another ex-cop. I like Henri a lot. She's an artist. She's kind of eccentric and is always interesting to spend time with. I've stayed with her plenty of times over the years, usually on weekends when my father had to work. He usually neglected to mention this to my mother, who thought that he should be able to arrange his life so that he could spend quality time with me every other weekend. I usually backed him up by keeping my mouth shut.

"Dad, I'm sixteen." Both of my parents seemed to be having trouble remembering this. "I can look after myself."

"I know you can. But I want you to stay with her anyway."

"Dad, come on! Weren't you ever young?"

"That's the problem, Robbie. I was. Hard as it is to imagine, I was once sixteen. Your mother would have my head if she found out I left you alone with a teenage boy—especially that particular teenage boy—in the same building."

"*Da*-ad!"

"Humor me, Robbie, okay?"

"But—"

"You know I never criticize your mother."

Surprisingly, considering that they're divorced, that's true. Sometimes he pokes fun at her, but he never says anything negative. Not to me, anyway.

"And you know we both work hard at making sure that our problems don't become your problems."

"Yes, but—"

"Your mother has reservations about Nick."

"She *told* you that?"

"She did. She called me last night, Robbie. She worries about you. She still hasn't gotten over the Trisha Carnegie thing."

Trisha was a girl who had gone missing. I'd helped to find her.

"She blames me for getting you involved," he said.

"But—"

"It scared her. Things could easily have turned out badly."

"But they didn't."

"I love you, Robbie," my father said. "I like that you can come around as often as you do. I like that you spend weekends here. I especially like that we manage to do it all in a relatively civilized manner. I'd like to keep it that way."

"So would I, Dad."

"So, do me—and your mother—a favor. Stay with Henri tonight, okay?"

"Okay," I said.

"If you need me, you can get me on my cell phone. Any time."

"*Okay*, Dad."

He dug his wallet out of his pocket and handed me some bills. I could tell even without counting that it was a lot of money. "You heard what Stan said," he said. "Christmas will be here before you know it. You might want to start looking for something for your mother. And Robbie? Be good." He sounded exactly like my mother, which would have surprised her. "I'll be in touch."

Meaning, he would check on me.

. . .

Nick led the way down the stairs. When we got outside, he said, "That was about me, right?"

"No, it wasn't."

"What then?"

"My dad has to go out of town, and my mom's away on a business trip, so he wants me to stay with Henri tonight."

"You need a *babysitter?*"

"Henri isn't a babysitter," I said. "She's a friend. It's just that he thinks my mother would be upset if she found out I stay here alone."

"Especially since I live right downstairs, right? He doesn't trust me, does he?" He sounded bitter.

"That's not it at all. He just worries about me, that's all."

"Right."

I stared up into his eyes. "He wants me to stay with Henri because of what happened with Trisha Carnegie," I said. "And because of how my mom reacted."

I couldn't tell whether or not Nick believed me, but he held my hand all the way to the bus stop. While we walked, his eyes never stopped moving—up the street, down the street, across the street.

"Expecting company?" I said as we reached the bus shelter.

"Huh?"

"You keep looking around. Like you're expecting someone."

"I'm just looking for the bus." He was lying. I knew it. I could tell by the way he avoided looking at me. "Here it comes." He started out of the bus shelter. When I didn't follow him immediately, he took me by the hand. While we waited for the bus to pull up in front of us, he said, "Hey, Robyn? I had a lousy week—work and school and everything. I just want us to have a good time today, okay?"

I said okay. I wondered what he meant by *everything*.

The bus lumbered to a stop. We climbed aboard, paid our fares, and headed to the back. Only after scanning every face in the bus did Nick sink into his seat. I snuggled against him, but I couldn't shake the feeling that something was wrong. Something he didn't want to tell me about—yet. Maybe if the day went well, he would open up. I decided to give him time to unwind.

"Where are we going?" I said.

"I thought maybe Chinatown."

"*Chinatown?*" There were lots of things to do in and around the city—movies, museums, art galleries (which, to be honest, I would never have expected Nick to suggest), maybe a walk in the park. But Chinatown?

"Have you been down there lately?" Nick said.

"I was only a couple of blocks from there when I was robbed this morning."

"Does that mean you don't want to go back?"

"No," I said. "I'm just a little surprised, that's all. You've never mentioned Chinatown before."

He shrugged. "There are lots of cool stores down there. I thought maybe I could find something for Jack for Christmas." Jack was Nick's baby nephew. "And we could have lunch at a Chinese restaurant. Hey, you want to go to the Santa Claus parade tomorrow?"

"The Santa Claus parade?" I couldn't picture Nick at a parade that attracted mainly little kids and their parents.

"What's the matter?" Nick said. "You don't need a little magic in your life?"

"*Christmas* magic, you mean?"

"Yeah. My mom used to take me to the parade every year. Then we'd go and stand in line at one of the malls so I could tell Santa what I wanted for Christmas. My mom always used to have my picture taken, you know, sitting on Santa's knee. She had a whole collection of those pictures, from when I was a little boy till I was maybe eight or nine years old."

So he was feeling nostalgic. Nick's mother had died a few years ago. Nick's stepfather was responsible. His stepfather was also responsible for the scar on Nick's face. He was in prison now. So was Nick's stepbrother, Joey. The only other family Nick had was his aunt and his nephew Jack, whom he had never seen in person. Joey's girlfriend had been pregnant when Joey went to prison. She moved out west to be with her family when she had the baby. All Nick had seen of Jack were a few pictures. And Christmas was on the way—the time of year when everybody thought about family. I squeezed Nick's hand.

"I haven't been to the Santa parade in years," I said. "Let's do it. It'll be fun."

We took the bus into the heart of the city. The Chinatown area is laid out like a big cross, running about ten city blocks east-west and eight city blocks north-south. Originally all of the restaurants and businesses had been Chinese. These days at least half of them are Vietnamese, but people still call the area as Chinatown.

Traffic always moves more slowly through China-town on weekends. People from all over flock to the area to check out the shops, eat at the restaurants, and socialize with friends. As soon as we got to the fringes of Chinatown, Nick leaned over me and pulled the cord to get off. We jumped down onto the street.

Making our way along the sidewalk was like navigating an obstacle course, even early in the morning. The contents of every store seemed to have spilled out onto the sidewalk. Rickety tables outside grocery stores were laden with fruits and vegetables, half of which I couldn't name. Racks and tables of clothing crowded the side-walks outside of clothing stores, displaying traditional Chinese garments as well as tourist T-shirts and sweat-shirts. Every few feet a double-parked truck blocked the narrow street while men unloaded crates onto what was left of the sidewalk, forcing passing pedestrians onto the street, which made things even more difficult for the cars trying to get by.

"Isn't it great here?" Nick said. "It's like another world."

It really was. All the stores and restaurants had English names painted on their signs and awnings. But they also had bigger, bolder Chinese or Vietnamese names. And most of the people—not all, but most—going in and out of the shops were of Chinese or Vietnamese descent. The younger people, the twentysomethings and the kids my age, all looked hip and trendy. But then you'd see old people, wrinkled grandfathers and tiny grandmothers, dressed in traditional-style pants and tunics.

Nick held my hand tightly as he wove his way through the crowd and the sidewalk tables.

"Let's get something to eat," Nick said. "I know this great bakery. And a good restaurant where we can have lunch a little later. And I thought this afternoon we could—what's the matter, Robyn? Why are you looking at me like that?"

"Because—I was thinking that you'd forgotten all about me. But I can see you've given a lot of thought to this weekend. It's kind of nice."

He smiled back at me and kissed me lightly on the lips. "I wasn't kidding, Robyn. I really missed you. It's just hard to work *and* keep up in school."

"It's okay," I said. "I'm just glad we're together now. Come on. Show me that bakery."

He led me down the street, around the corner, and into a brightly lit store that was obviously popular. It was thronged with customers. Everyone in the place, except Nick and me, was Asian. No one was speaking English.

"Take a look around," Nick said. "Maybe you'll find something you can take to Henri's later."

"Good idea," I said.

I had to peek around all the customers to see the display cases. I recognized some of the items—sponge cake, coconut cake, egg-custard tarts, almond cookies, apple turnovers. But I had no idea what other items were. I had to rely on the little labels on each tray. There were also sesame balls, crispy honey butterflies, and bright yellow biscuits called "sunny cookies." Everything looked so good—okay, so I wasn't too sure about the egg custard—that I couldn't make up my mind. I looked around for Nick.

I couldn't see him anywhere.

I doubled back to the bakery's main door, scanning the customers as I went. Normally Nick is easy to spot in a crowd because of his jet-black hair. But everyone in the bakery besides me had black hair. I finally caught sight of him standing at a display case near the front of the store.

I began to work my way toward him. It wasn't easy. People were pressed close to the display cases, giving what sounded like complicated orders to the counter attendants. No one seemed to want to move for fear of losing their places.

I kept my eyes on Nick as I picked my way through all the people and saw a counter attendant, a pretty Chinese girl, say something to him. Nick pointed to something in the display case and held up two fingers. The girl's head disappeared for a moment and then bobbed up again. I saw her slip two pastries into a brown paper bag. She said something else to Nick. He shook his head.

The girl threaded her way through the other counter attendants toward the cash register. Nick followed her on the other side of the display case. He handed something to her—payment for his order. As she opened the cash drawer, she made a quick scan of the crowded store. Nick glanced around too. Then the girl reached down under the counter. She continued to check out the customers and her coworkers as she fiddled with the bag containing Nick's pastries. She folded the top of the bag and handed it to Nick along with his change.

They looked at each other for a moment. Nick didn't move, even though he had already paid. Then someone shouted and the girl jumped. She had a startled look on her face, as if she had just been caught doing something she had been told not to do. She called something in Chinese to the woman who had shouted at her, then she hurried away. Nick watched her go. When he backed away from the counter, his eyes were still on the girl. I squeezed through the crowd toward him. He took my hand and led me out into the street.

"Who was that?" I said.

"Who was who?"

"That girl."

"What girl?"

"The girl behind the counter," I said.

He looked baffled. "What do you mean? She's just a girl who works there."

"But you know her, right?"

"What makes you think that?"

"Come on. I saw the way she was looking at you. Did she slip you an extra pastry, Nick?" I made a grab for the bag he was carrying.

Nick swung it up out of my reach.

"You think she was checking me out?" he said, grinning. "What's the matter? Are you jealous, Robyn?"

"So you *don't* know her?"

Nick's grin widened. He seemed to be enjoying this. "Yeah, you're jealous," he said. He ducked to kiss me on the lips. "I've never had anyone jealous on account of me before."

"I am *not* jealous," I said. Okay, that wasn't completely honest. I had definitely felt a twinge when I'd seen the way the girl had looked at Nick. She was so pretty—petite, lively dark eyes, long, glossy black hair. But the girl wasn't the only thing that was bothering me. Something was going on with Nick. He didn't usually scout his surroundings the way he had done before we got on the bus—and the way he was doing again now that we had left the bakery. His eyes were moving all the time, checking faces on the sidewalk and on the other side of the street, skimming the road and the cars going in both directions, taking a good look around before turning a corner. And then there was that bruise on his neck . . .

When I'd met Nick at the animal shelter a few months back, he had been doing time on a conviction for property damage and assault. It wasn't the first time he had been in trouble. But he had been trying to change. He had worked hard to make sure that when he finished his time, he would never have to go back. He had been looking forward to living with his aunt, maybe getting a dog. Nick loves dogs. But Glen, his aunt's new boyfriend, didn't like Nick, so it hadn't worked out. Nick had been disappointed, but he was still trying. He was living on his own, going to school, holding down a steady job, and he had a part-time gig walking a couple of dogs. I had thought that everything was going to turn out okay. Until our trip to Chinatown. He was acting strangely. And that worried me.

Nick and I had gone a whole block before I said, "I thought you were hungry. Aren't you going to eat that?"

Nick gave me a blank look. I nodded at the paper bakery bag he was carrying.

"Oh, yeah," he said. "I was just looking for a place where we could sit down. How 'bout that mall over there?" He pointed down the street. "I'll buy you some tea."

"Okay."

Nick held my hand as we crossed the street, and that made me feel better. It always did. We made our way through the mall's lower level until we ended up in a food court.

"You stay here," Nick said, pointing to an empty table. "I'll get us something to drink. You want Chinese tea or regular?"

"Chinese."

Still carrying his bakery bag, Nick bounded across the court to a counter on the far side and waited until the woman behind the counter had finished serving another customer. She turned to Nick and he placed his order. The woman reached for a couple of cups—one with a Coke logo on it and the other one a sturdier, card-board cup for hot drinks. But instead of filling them, she disappeared through a door behind the counter.

When she emerged a moment later, with both cups still in her hand, a man followed her. He was wearing a white apron and had a white cap on his head. He lifted a plastic tray off a stack near the cash register and set it on the counter. The woman poured hot water into the cardboard cup, and the man filled the other cup with Coke for Nick. While the woman put lids on the cups, Nick moved to the cash register and dug in his pocket for money to pay for the drinks. He handed it to the man. Maybe he used too many small coins, or maybe he gave the man the wrong amount, because the man stared at whatever was in his hand for a few moments. He looked up at Nick and frowned. Finally he stepped over to the cash register. Nick moved with the man. The man handed him something—his change, I guess—and Nick put it in his pocket. He dropped the bakery bag onto the tray with the drinks and headed back across the food court toward me.

"Here you are," he said, taking one of the cups off the tray and sliding it across the table to me. "One cup of Chinese tea."

"Was there a problem?" I said.

"What do you mean?" He sat down, peeled the plastic lid off his Coke, and took a long gulp.

"The man at the register—he was looking at you funny."

"What do you mean?"

"You didn't notice?"

He shook his head. "First you think the girl at the bakery was looking at me funny. Now it's the man at the cash. You know what I think, Robyn? I think you should have stayed in bed this morning instead of picking up dead birds. You could have used the extra sleep." He opened the bakery bag, took out two round, flat pastries, and grinned appreciatively. "Mmmmm. Red bean paste," he said. "Want to try one?"

"*Bean* paste?" I shook my head.

"Have you ever tried it?" Nick said.

"Well, no."

Nick broke off a piece of pastry and held it out to me. When I started to protest, he said, "What's the matter? Don't you trust me?"

"Yes, but—"

"It's really good. I wouldn't lie to you, Robyn." He pushed the piece of pastry closer to me. With a sigh, I accepted it and took a tiny bite.

"Well?" Nick said.

It didn't taste at all the way I thought something called red bean paste would. In fact, it tasted really good. I took another bite. Before I knew it, I had eaten the whole piece. Nick took the second pastry from the bag, broke it in half, and gave a piece to me. I ate it with my tea.

When we had finished, I put our empty cups onto the tray and reached for the bag the pastries had been in. Nick snatched it from me and eased the tray out of my hand.

"I'll take care of that," he said. He got up and carried the tray to the trash. He slid the cups into the slot, but not the bakery bag. Instead, he carefully folded it and slipped it into one of his hoodie's big front pockets, scanning the food court but trying to appear casual about it.

"Is everything okay?" I said when he came back to the table to get me.

He looked at me for a moment as if it were a crazy question.

"Sure," he said. "Why wouldn't it be?"

That was my question exactly.

CHAPTER **FIVE**

We spent the morning visiting stores, checking out imported toys, fans, peacock feathers, silk purses, embroidered jackets, beautiful jade jewelry and statues—the dragons were my favorite—kites, bamboo furniture, and scrolls painted with cherry blossoms. Every now and then I'd turn to say something to Nick, but he wouldn't be there. Then he would turn up again, take my hand in his, and kiss my cheek, acting like a guy who was enjoying his first weekend off in a very long time.

Finally he said, "I'm starving. You ready for lunch?"

As a matter of fact, I was. I had been up since four and hadn't eaten anything except some pieces of bean paste pastry.

The restaurant Nick wanted to eat at was located off the main roads, tucked halfway up a narrow side street.

"It's not fancy, but the food is terrific," he said.

Nick was right. The place didn't look like much on the outside—a low, grime-stained brick building with a red-and-white sign. The small English lettering said "Golden Treasures." The dining room inside was tiny, the tables were covered with red plastic tablecloths, and the chairs were mismatched. Nick led me to a table for two along one wall and helped me out of my jacket. A woman approached us with a pot of tea and a couple of menus. She filled the little handle-less teacups on the table and handed us each a menu. I opened it and was relieved to find that it was written in both Chinese and English.

"I have a few suggestions, if you're interested," Nick said.

I let him order, which turned out to be a good decision. Within twenty minutes we were sampling our first dish. The restaurant started to fill around us. All of the other customers appeared to be Chinese.

"That tells you something about the place," Nick said. "If Chinese people eat here, you know you're getting authentic Chinese food."

"What does that say about the cuisine at McDonald's?" I said. "That it's authentic North American food?"

Nick laughed. "They have McDonald's in Europe and in Russia now. I think they even have McDonald's in China. Do you think that means it's authentic *global* food?" He poured me another cup of tea from the pot the woman had left on the table. We dug into a platter of shrimp, another of chicken in black bean sauce, and a dish of stir-fried vegetables. I couldn't believe how hungry I was.

"You want the last of the chicken?" Nick said finally.

"Are you kidding? If I eat another bite, I'll explode."

"Me too," Nick said. But that didn't stop him from polishing off the remains of the chicken and the last of the shrimp. When he had cleaned all of the platters, he raised a hand and signaled the woman. She brought our bill and a couple of fortune cookies. Nick took one, broke it open, and grinned at me.

"'Love will bless your day,'" he said. Maybe he didn't think I believed him because he handed me the little slip of paper so I could read it myself. "What does yours say?"

I cracked open my fortune cookie and pulled out a slip of paper. "'Be careful who you trust.'" I glanced across the table at him. "Good thing I don't believe in fortunes."

Nick popped his cookie into his mouth and was chewing happily when I noticed an older Chinese man staring at him from the door to the kitchen.

Nick must have caught my expression. "Something wrong?" he said.

I nodded at the kitchen door. Nick turned. The Chinese man met Nick's eyes and held them a moment before disappearing back into the kitchen.

"What do you think that was about?" I said.

Nick shrugged. He took out his wallet.

"Lunch is on me," I said.

"No way, Robyn. I invited you."

I'd been going to argue, but he was already shaking his head. He put some money down on top of the bill and slipped his hoodie on. "Why don't you think about what you want to do next?" he said, standing up. "I'll be right back."

"Where are you . . ."

He nodded to a sign for the restrooms. As he left the main dining room, I decided I should also probably go. I'd had a lot of tea. I got up and walked toward the signs. The restrooms were down a long corridor off the dining room. But as I turned into that corridor, I saw Nick leaving the restaurant through the emergency exit at the far end.

"Hey!" I said. But the door had already clanged shut behind him. I ran after him—but stopped when I heard someone shouting behind me. A man ran toward me. "Do not use," he said, pushing past me and blocking my exit. "Fire door only."

"But—"

He shook his head no.

I hurried back to the main room, pulled on my jacket, and dashed outside. A narrow alley ran along the side of the restaurant. I followed it to the rear of the building where Nick had exited. I didn't see him anywhere. I went to the door that I was pretty sure he had come out of and tried it, but it wouldn't open from the outside— he couldn't have gone back that way.

I glanced around. The alley continued for a couple of blocks between the backs of stores on one side and the backs of houses on the other. But where was Nick? Why had he ducked out on me like that?

Then I heard a voice. It was low, but I was pretty sure it was Nick's. It sounded like he was just up the alley somewhere. I headed toward the sound. It was coming from the other side of a high, gated fence. I crept toward it. No way to peek through—it was a privacy fence—but the gate was partially open. I squinted through the small crack and saw Nick. He was in a tiny yard that was laid out as a garden—a vegetable garden, I guessed, from the stakes that stood in rows in the cold early November soil. Nick was standing on the path, taking something—a white envelope—from the old man I had seen in the restaurant. He tucked the envelope into a hoodie pocket. The old man said something to him. Nick nodded. He began to turn, probably to make his way back to the restaurant.

I darted away from the gate, suddenly ashamed that I had been spying on him, and ran back toward the restaurant. Just as I got there, two men stepped out of the kitchen and into the alley. They were both wearing sunglasses and dark suit jackets. They stared at me and then started up the alley toward me. I slowed my pace and told myself not to be nervous. It was broad daylight. What could possibly happen?

The two men blocked my way. Neither stepped aside to let me pass.

"Excuse me," I said.

They looked around, as if they were expecting to see someone else in the alley with me.

"What are you doing back here?" one of them said.

"I'm meeting someone," I said. Not that it was any of their business.

The man who had spoken glanced around. "I don't see anyone," he said. He took a long, hard look at me. "What were you doing up there?" he said, stepping closer, crowding me the way bullies do. I felt like jelly inside. Whoever these guys were, they were scary.

"I really have to go," I said. I hoped they didn't hear the tremor in my voice. What were *they* doing back here? I was getting ready to run—maybe even scream if I had to—when someone behind them said something in Chinese. It was the same old man who had been in the yard with Nick just a few minutes before. He had somehow managed to get back into the restaurant without passing me. He must have gone out through the front of the yard and circled the block. But why?

The two men turned to look at the old man. The guy who had been doing all the talking said something to him. Then I heard someone call my name. I turned and saw Nick standing on the sidewalk near the front of the restaurant. He and the old man must have come back together.

The two men looked at Nick. They must have decided that I was telling the truth because they stepped aside to let me pass. Then one of them said something to the old man. The old man shook his head. The guy who had been doing all the talking moved closer to the old man, trying to bully him the same way he had bullied me. The old man stayed exactly where he was. Finally the two guys muscled past him into the restaurant. The old man remained in the doorway, looking at me.

A moment later, Nick was by my side.

"What are you doing out here, Robyn?" he said. He didn't even look at the old man. You would never have guessed that they had been talking together just a few minutes ago. He took my hand and led me out to the sidewalk, away from the restaurant. "When I went back to the table, you were gone. Why didn't you wait for me?"

"I was looking for you," I said.

"Looking for me? You knew where I was going. I told you I'd be right back."

I was trying to decide whether I should confront him with what I had just seen when: "Hey!"

No sooner had we stepped out onto the sidewalk than he yanked me back into the alley, pressed me up against the wall, and kissed me. At first I was so startled that I resisted. But I couldn't help it—I kissed him back. My heart pounded in my chest. I couldn't think of anywhere else I'd rather be, anything else I'd rather be doing, or anyone else I'd rather be with. When Nick finally pulled away, he said, "I've been thinking about doing that all day." He smiled down at me. His hoodie was half unzipped, leaving part of his neck bare. I reached up and touched the black and blue bruise on the side of it. He winced. For a moment I forgot about him slipping out of the restaurant.

"What happened, Nick?"

He brought his face down close to mine and kissed me again.

"I don't want to talk about that," he murmured.

I wanted to talk about it. I also wanted to talk about what had just happened. But if I pushed him, the mood would be ruined. I told myself it could wait. We had all weekend.

We snuggled for a few more minutes. Finally Nick said, "So, did you decide what you want to do?"

"How about a movie?" I said. "My treat." I was tired. It would be nice to be able to sit down for a few hours and maybe rest my head on Nick's shoulder. "We can get a paper and see what's playing."

"Sounds good," he said. We were holding hands again when we stepped back out onto the street. "There's a box of those free weeklies over there," Nick said, nodding toward the main intersection. When we reached the corner, he said, "You get check the listings. Pick something you want to see. I'll meet you back here in a couple of minutes."

"Where are you going?"

"I have to do something. I'll be right back. I promise." The walk sign had switched to an orange hand. Nick jogged into the intersection before I could say another word.

I started to follow him but the light turned red. I stood on the edge of the sidewalk and watched him. When he reached the other side, he stopped in front of the first store on the block. A man was standing outside, smoking a cigarette. He threw it down and crushed it under his heel when Nick pushed the door open. The man followed Nick inside.

I watched them through the store's plate-glass window. Nick was standing at the front of the store, picking things up and putting them back down again. The other man circled around behind the counter. *He must be the owner*, I thought, *or maybe a store clerk*.

Nick disappeared from sight for a moment. When he came back, he put something on the counter. The man went to the cash register and Nick paid him. The man put Nick's purchase in a small bag, then reached for something else under the counter. Nick's back was blocking the man from view, but I was pretty sure that the man was giving Nick whatever he had reached for.

As Nick turned away, I saw him put something in his pocket. I started to get a sick feeling in my stomach. Whatever Nick was up to, he didn't want me to know about. I wondered if it had anything to do with the way he had reacted when Stan Rogers had showed up at my father's place. Despite what Nick had said, I was pretty sure that he hadn't just seen Stan around. Nick knew him. Maybe he had even had a run-in with him, which would explain the way Stan had looked at Nick.

I also wondered what my father knew—whether he had a reason he hadn't told me for wanting me to stay at Henri's. I waited impatiently for the light to change. Maybe Nick didn't want to talk about what was going on. Maybe forcing him to talk was going to ruin the whole day. But I didn't care about that anymore. I wanted answers.

Nick came out of the store and walked back to the corner. A steady stream of cars whizzed by him while he waited for the light to change. When he spotted me waiting on the other side of the street, he smiled and waved a hand. People gathered around him—other pedestrians, waiting for the light to change. I saw a couple of them frown as a tall, blond-haired guy suddenly started to shove his way through them toward the curb. *Some people are so rude*, I thought. Then, just like that, it happened.

I gasped. I couldn't believe what I was seeing.

Nick lurched forward. I couldn't figure out why. What was he doing? Then I saw the startled look on his face. He turned his head, even as he was staggering forward, his arms pinwheeling frantically in the air. He was falling out into the street.

I heard the squeal of brakes. Then—*ohmygod!* I wanted to close my eyes but I couldn't look away. Nick must have seen the same thing I saw—a car was almost on top of him. Then came the impact and a sickening thud. Nick flew up onto the hood just as the car rocked to a stop. When he rolled back down again, I heard the *bang, bang, bang* of a chain reaction as another car crashed into the first car, then a third car hit the second one and another one hit that car. Traffic stopped in all directions. People crowded into the street. I ran toward Nick.

When I reached him, he wasn't moving.

CHAPTER **SIX**

As far as I could tell, Nick wasn't even breathing. The driver of the car, a tense, terrified-looking middle-aged woman, had struggled out from behind the wheel and was staring down at him, her face white. She was shaking all over.

"He jumped out in front of me," she said.

I sank to my knees beside Nick. Tears were running down my cheeks and there was nothing I could do to stop them. He was so still. I couldn't see any movement in his chest, not even the smallest up and down from the shallowest of breathing. I forced myself to think. *What do you do in an emergency?* I was supposed to know. I had taken a first aid course when I was twelve years old. It had been my mother's idea—of course. *Think, Robyn.*

First, check for a pulse.

I pressed a finger to the side of Nick's neck and located a pulse. *Thank you, thank you, thank you.*

Next, get help.

I looked up at the people who were crowded around. "Someone call 9-1-1," I said.

A man was already on his cell phone. "I'm making the call right now," he said.

Something caught my eye behind him. The tall blond guy. He was staring down at Nick. When he looked up again, I saw something hard and cold in his eyes. Then—I was sure of it—he smiled. A tight, nasty little smile. He started to turn away.

"Hey!" I shouted. I stood up just as he melted into the crowd. I wanted to go after him. I wanted to grab him and ask him what he was smiling about. But I couldn't leave Nick.

"He just jumped out in front of me," the driver said again. "I tried to stop, but he jumped out in front of me." She swayed on her feet.

"Someone help me!" I said, grabbing her around the waist. "I think she's going to faint."

The man who had called 9-1-1 took the woman by the arm and asked her if she was all right. Then he steered her back to her car. Over his shoulder he said to me, "An ambulance is on its way. So are the police."

In the distance I heard a siren.

I knelt down beside Nick.

Behind me, someone was ordering the crowd to "Step aside, people. Step aside." I turned and saw a police officer making his way to where Nick was lying. A police car pulled up, blocking oncoming cars, and another cop got out and started to unsnarl the traffic clogging the intersection.

The first police officer looked around. "Can someone tell me what happened here?" he said.

While the man who had called 9-1-1 was filling him in, an ambulance nosed through the congestion. Two paramedics got out and knelt beside Nick. One of them felt for a pulse. The other one asked me what had happened.

I thought I could stay calm while I told him. I knew it was important for the paramedics to have as much information as possible. But when I opened my mouth to speak, I started to sob.

"I know you're upset," the paramedic said. He had a soft but firm voice. "But it would be a big help if you could give us as much information as possible."

I sucked in a deep breath and told him everything while his partner checked Nick's blood pressure.

"Is he a friend of yours?" the paramedic said.

I nodded.

"Do you know if he has any special medical conditions or any allergies?"

I said I didn't think so, but that I didn't know for sure. He asked me a lot more questions about Nick, most of which I couldn't answer.

The paramedics talked among themselves for a moment. Then one of them went to the ambulance and came back with a rolling stretcher and a long board.

"We're going to immobilize him," said the paramedic who had asked me all the questions. He and his partner slid the board under Nick and strapped him to it. Then they lifted Nick onto the stretcher and wheeled him toward the ambulance. One of the paramedics told the police which hospital they were taking him to. After the ambulance left, an officer said to me, "I understand you know the victim."

I nodded.

He asked me Nick's full name, age, address, and phone number. "We'll need to contact his parents," he said.

"He doesn't have any parents."

"Well, then, whoever is responsible for him."

"He lives alone," I said. "But he has an aunt in the city." He wrote down her name and the address I gave him. I said I didn't know her phone number.

"Did you see what happened?" he said.

I fumbled in my pocket for some tissues. Tears were trickling down my cheeks again and I needed to blow my nose. But—it figured—I couldn't find what I was looking for. I sniffed loudly. The man who called 9-1-1 reached out and pressed a couple of tissues into my hand.

"I have to go to the hospital," I told the police officer. "I have to see him."

For a moment, I thought he was going to argue with me. Then he closed his notebook and said, "We'll take you there. We'll see how he is. Then we're going to want to ask you some questions, okay?"

I said okay. I would have agreed to anything so long as I got to the hospital.

．　．　．

The hospital wasn't far from the scene of the accident. When we got there, the two police officers went inside with me. One of them asked about Nick at the emergency department's information desk. But it was too soon. All they could find out was that Nick had arrived and that he was being examined.

One of the officers led me to a corner of the waiting room while the other one went to contact Nick's aunt. The police officer who stayed with me asked if I wanted anything to drink. When I said I didn't, he sat down next to me and spent the next twenty minutes reviewing the accident with me. After I told him everything I could remember, he asked me more questions. He wanted to know exactly where I had been standing and exactly what I had seen. "Not what you *think* happened, Robyn, but what you saw with your own eyes." He asked if I had any idea what made Nick leap out into traffic. I said I didn't. Then I said, "I think he might have been pushed."

The officer regarded me calmly, just like my father always did when I said something unexpected.

"What makes you say that?" he said.

I started to say that I wasn't sure. And it was true, I wasn't. Except: "Nick was waiting for the light to turn," I said. "He waved to me. He looked happy." I had a clear picture in my mind of Nick at the edge of the curb, looking across the street at me. "Then, all of a sudden, he sort of stumbled forward. I saw a surprised look on his face. I thought someone must have bumped into him." I remembered the tall blond guy and the cold look on his face when he saw Nick lying on the road. "But now I'm not so sure that's what happened," I said. "There was this guy." I described him as best I could—which turned out to be not much of a description. All I could say for certain was that he had seemed taller than Nick, he had longish blond hair and blue eyes, and he was wearing a dark green leather jacket. In other words, just one more body in the crowd. In a city this size, he would be difficult to find, assuming the police even decided to look.

"Did you recognize him?" the police officer said. "Have you seen him before?"

I shook my head.

"Do you know if your boyfriend knows him?"

I said I didn't.

"Do you have any idea why this person—or anyone else—would push your boyfriend into traffic?"

"No."

"Has your boyfriend been in any trouble that you know of?"

I hesitated.

"Robyn?" he said. "If you know anything that could be useful . . ."

"He's been in trouble before," I said. "But that was a long time ago." I told him a little about Nick's background.

"We'll have to talk to him," he said. "Would you recognize this person again if you saw him?"

"I'm not sure," I said. "I think so."

The police officer closed his notebook and said he was going to check on Nick's condition. He had just returned to tell me that there was no news when I spotted Nick's Aunt Beverly outside the ER entrance with two other officers. One was the police officer who had gone to telephone her. The other was Glen Ross, her boyfriend. They talked together for a few minutes before they came inside. The officer who was with me went to join them.

While they talked, the police officer who had been with me took out his notebook and started writing again. He glanced at me. The look on his face told me that good old Glen was filling them in on Nick's past—and that what he was saying was different from what I had said. That's when Nick's aunt noticed me. She left Glen with the other two officers and came to sit beside me.

"They told me Nick was hit by a car." Her voice was shaky and her eyes were red. "They say there's no news yet."

I almost started crying again but forced myself to stay calm.

"They said he might have been pushed," she said. "Was he in a fight?"

"No," I said. "It wasn't his fault. He didn't do anything."

"But you told the police that you saw someone push him. He must have done something. It's always something with Nick."

"He didn't do anything," I said again. Then I back-tracked a little. "I'm not one hundred percent sure what happened," I said. "I was on the other side of the street. I just told the police that from where I was standing, it looked like he might have been pushed. Nick will be able to tell them for sure."

Glen broke away from the other officers and went to the information desk. I held my breath and tried to read the expression on his face, but it was impossible. Finally he came over to where we were waiting. He sat down beside Nick's aunt and took one of her hands into his.

"They're going to tell us the minute they know any-thing," he said. His voice sounded almost gentle, which surprised me. The only time I had met Glen, he and Nick had been in a fight and Glen had gotten physical. I had taken an immediate dislike to him. He looked at me now. "It's Robyn, right?"

I nodded.

"I know your father."

I already knew that. My father had told me that Glen was a good cop. He'd also said that he wasn't surprised that Glen and Nick didn't get along. According to my father, a lot of cops get used to being in charge. But Nick didn't like to be ordered around. Another problem, ac-cording to my father, was that Glen had probably seen too many kids like Nick, and Nick had had too many run-ins with cops. They were predisposed to dislike each other.

"I understand you were with Nick when it happened," Glen said.

"Robyn says it was an accident," Nick's aunt said.

I stared at her. That wasn't what I had said at all.

"I'd like to hear it from Robyn," Glen said. He turned back to me. "They said you told them Nick was pushed. Who'd he piss off this time?"

I glanced at Nick's aunt. She was shaking her head.

"Robyn?" Glen said. "You saw the whole thing. What happened? Did someone push him or not?"

"I—I don't know," I said. But when I replayed the scene in my mind, I couldn't shake the feeling that he had been pushed. "It happened so fast. One minute he was on the curb, the next he was on the street. I thought he must have been pushed, but now I don't know. He didn't do anything. Why would anyone push him when he was just standing there minding his own business?"

"Maybe he mouthed off to someone. You know how that kid can be," Glen said. He glanced at Nick's aunt.

She nodded unhappily.

"Or maybe he was trying to cross against the light," Glen said. "You have any idea how many kids I see doing that every day?"

I didn't know what to say. Glen seemed genuinely concerned about Nick's aunt, but he hadn't changed at all where Nick was concerned.

Glen stood up. "I could use a coffee," he said. "You want one, Bev?" She nodded. "What about you, Robyn?"

I said no thanks.

After he'd gone, a woman came over and asked Nick's aunt about her relationship to Nick. She said there were forms that had to be filled out. She handed Nick's aunt a clipboard and a pen.

Glen was on his way back with coffee when the woman behind the information desk pointed him out to a man in a white lab coat with a stethoscope around his neck. A doctor. When Nick's aunt saw the doctor talking to Glen, she stood up and went over to him. I trailed after her.

"—extremely lucky," the doctor was saying. "His left ankle is broken. He's got a lot of bumps and bruises. He also got a nasty bang on the head when he hit the pavement. We've x-rayed him, and we want to keep an eye on him to make sure he didn't get a serious concussion. But other than that . . ." He shrugged. "He's lucky that the car wasn't going fast. It could have been much worse."

"Can I see him?" Nick's aunt said.

"Certainly," the doctor said. "They're just taking him up to a room." He told us what the room number was.

Nick's aunt looked at me. "Do you want to come too, Robyn?" she said.

I nodded.

"Ms. Thrasher?" A woman came over to Nick's aunt and introduced herself as the person in charge of admissions. "I have a few more questions that I need you to answer, if you don't mind."

"You go ahead, Robyn," Nick's aunt said. "Tell Nick I'll be up to see him in a few minutes."

Glen stayed with Nick's aunt. I took the elevator up to the third floor and wandered through a maze of corridors until I reached Nick's room. There were two beds in it. An old man, either asleep or unconscious, occupied the one nearest to the door. Nick's bed was next to the window. A half-pulled curtain between the two beds divided the room. Nick's left leg, lying above the covers, was in a cast from his knee to his toes. He had a nasty scrape on one cheek, but he managed a smile when he saw me.

"I need you to do something for me, Robyn," he said before I could even ask how he was. "I need you to find out what they did with my clothes."

"Nick, what happened? I saw this guy—"

"I need my clothes right now, Robyn."

"But I saw—"

"*Now*, Robyn. Please?"

"Okay, but when I come back—"

"When you come back, we'll talk. I promise."

Nick's aunt entered the room just as I was leaving. Glen was with her, but he stayed outside in the hall.

"How is he?" he said.

"Okay, I guess," I said. "I just have to—" *Should I tell Glen that Nick had asked for his clothes?* I thought. *Would Nick want Glen to know?* "I'll be back in a minute," I said. I hurried off to find someone who could tell me what had happened to Nick's clothes.

A harried-looking nurse referred me to an orderly, who hunted around behind the nursing station and then handed me a big brown paper bag. I thanked him and headed back to Nick's room. Glen wasn't standing outside anymore, and Nick's aunt was still inside the room with Nick. I didn't want to intrude, so I took a seat in the small waiting area just down the hall. While I waited, I opened the brown bag to make sure that none of Nick's things had gone missing. Boots. Jeans. T-shirt. Hooded sweatshirt. Wallet. The small paper bag Nick had been carrying when he'd been hit. Inside was a wooden train—hand-painted, according to the box. I guessed it was a present for his nephew. I was putting it back when I saw something else at the bottom of the big bag the orderly had given me. A thick envelope. It must have fallen out of Nick's hoodie.

I told myself that whatever was in it was none of my business. But I kept staring at it. Nick had been acting strangely all day. So had some of the people I had seen him with, like the girl in the bakery and the man at the food court.

I hesitated. I told myself it was wrong to snoop. But I couldn't help myself. I opened the envelope—and gasped.

The envelope was stuffed with money. I thumbed the bills. They added up to hundreds of dollars. There were also six thinner envelopes inside. Five of them were folded shut, but not sealed. I checked them one by one. They all contained money. The sixth envelope was sealed, so I couldn't look inside. It felt different from the others. Maybe there was more money in it, but there was also something else.

We had gone into a lot of stores that morning. In some of them, Nick had disappeared from sight for a few minutes, sometimes for longer. He must have ducked out of sight to collect envelopes and money. In other places, I had been able to watch what was happening even if I didn't understand it. At the bakery, I had seen the girl at the register reach under the counter for something that she had slipped into Nick's bag. At the food court, Nick had blocked my view of the register when he paid for our drinks, but I had seen him put something into his pocket. And I was pretty sure that the man in the last store Nick had been in had handed him something besides the wood train.

What was going on?

Someone said my name, and I jumped. Nick's aunt was walking toward me. I slipped the envelope full of money into my purse as calmly as I could and stood up.

"He wants to see you," she said. "Glen went to tell the police that they can see Nick. They'll want to ask him some questions. I'll give you some time alone with him, Robyn. I'll be back in a little while."

I went back into the room with the big brown paper bag containing Nick's clothes. Nick grabbed the bag from my hands, pulled out his hooded sweatshirt, and pawed through the front pockets. When he came up empty, he dumped the contents of the bag onto the bed and started to root frantically through them.

I pulled the thick envelope out of my purse.

"Is this what you're looking for?" I said.

For a moment, Nick looked relieved. Then he caught the expression on my face.

"It's not what you think," he said.

CHAPTER **SEVEN**

"You have no idea what I think," I said.

"Are you kidding?" Nick said. "I know exactly what you think. Right now you look like every youth worker who's ever been assigned to me. You think I screwed up again," he said.

"There's a lot of money in this envelope, Nick."

"I didn't steal it, if that's what you're worried about." He held out his hand. "Give it to me, Robyn."

I put the envelope back into my purse.

"Most of the places we went today, someone gave you money, correct?" I said.

Nick made a face. "Now you look like your mother," he said. "But you sound like your father."

I crossed my arms over my chest and waited for an answer.

"Come on, Robyn. Hand it over."

"No. Not until you tell me why people have been giving you money."

"I can't."

"Does it have anything to do with the guy who pushed you?"

"*What?*" He looked and sounded genuinely surprised. "What guy? What are you talking about?"

"There was a guy standing behind you when you were waiting for the light to change. There was something funny about the way he was looking at you. He pushed you, didn't he, Nick?"

"I felt something," Nick said. He was frowning now. "Someone banged into me, hard. I lost my balance. But I thought it was an accident."

"I got a good look at him," I said. "He stuck around for a few seconds after that car hit you. And Nick? When he saw you lying in the street, he smiled." I shuddered at the memory. "I told the police—"

He stiffened. "You talked to the cops?"

"You were hit by a car. Someone called 9-1-1. The cops showed up. They wanted to know what happened. Of course I talked to them. I told them about the guy I saw—"

"What exactly did you tell them?"

I repeated the information I had given to the police.

"What did this guy look like?"

"He was tall. Taller than you, anyway. He had blond hair."

"*Blond* hair?" He reacted as if this was the last thing he'd expected me to say. "So he wasn't Chinese?"

"No. He had blond hair and blue eyes and a long, thin face." I was pretty sure I saw a flicker of recognition. "Do you know who he is, Nick?"

"*You're* the one who saw him, Robyn."

He was being evasive—not a good sign.

"You're telling me that you don't know anyone who looks like the guy I just described?"

"There must be thousands of people in this city with blond hair and blue eyes," Nick said.

"So the answer is no, you don't know any blond-haired, blue-eyed people who would want to push you into traffic?"

"No."

Nick isn't always cooperative. He doesn't always volunteer the whole truth and nothing but the truth. Sometimes he even lies. But he didn't fool me. Not in his hospital room, anyway. I had seen too much.

"Nick, what's going on? Tell me."

He looked at me for a moment. "Okay," he said in a low voice. He glanced toward the door and waved for me to come closer to him. As soon as I was beside the bed, he snatched my purse and dug out the envelope. He opened it and checked to see that everything was still there.

"Fine, have it your way," I said. "The police are on their way here to talk to you. They're going to ask you about that guy."

"And I'll tell them that I didn't see any guy and I don't know anything about being pushed. Someone bumped into me and I lost my balance, that's all."

"What if I tell them about all that money—"

I heard footsteps behind me and turned to see Nick's aunt entering the room. "There are two police officers here to see you, Nick," she said. "Can I bring them in?"

"In a sec," Nick said. "Just give me another minute with Robyn."

Nick's aunt nodded. As soon as she left the room, Nick began to stuff his clothes back into the big paper bag. He paused and looked at his jeans. One of the legs was ruined—it looked as if it had been cut open so the doctor could get a good look at his ankle or maybe get his jeans off over the swelling. Nick shook his head as he folded the pants and put them back into the bag. He started to put the envelope in too, then changed his mind.

"I need you to do something else for me, Robyn," he said.

Right. He felt free to ask me for favors, but he refused to tell me anything.

"Hang onto this," he said. He handed me the envelope. "I don't think it'll be safe in here, and I don't want anything to happen to it." I stared at it, but didn't take it. "Please, Robyn?" he said. "Trust me, okay?"

Trust someone who had been looking over his shoulder all day? Someone who, for some reason he wouldn't tell me, had been collecting money from storekeepers all day? Someone who was pretending he didn't know anything about a guy who had pushed him into traffic?

Trust someone who was begging me with purple-blue eyes that made me go weak in the knees? Someone who had held me and kissed me and whispered how much he had missed me?

"How about *you* trust *me*?" I said.

"I do trust you. I wouldn't be asking you to keep this for me if I didn't."

"What I mean is, how about trusting me enough to tell me what's going on?"

"As soon as I can, I will," he said. "I promise."

When I reluctantly reached for the envelope, he took my hand and pulled me gently toward him. He continued to tug until my face was close to his. Then he kissed me. "I promise," he said.

"When I saw that car hit you—"

"I'm fine." He kissed me again and didn't stop until someone rapped on the doorframe. It was his aunt. "Just a second," Nick said. He looked at me again. "Do me a favor?"

"*Another* favor, you mean."

"There's something at my place that I need. It's in a plastic bag on the kitchen counter. Can you get it for me? And while you're there, can you also get me another pair of jeans?"

"Sure," I said. "I'll bring them tomorrow."

"I need them now."

"What for? The doctor said they were keeping you here overnight. They want to make sure you don't have a concussion."

"Please, Robyn? The plastic bag on the counter. And some jeans. There's a pair in my closet." He dug into the bag and pulled a set of keys from his pants pocket. "Right away, okay?"

I glanced at the door, where his aunt was waiting. Then I took the keys and tucked the envelope back into my purse.

"I'll be back as soon as I can," I said.

He grinned for the first time since the accident. "I'm not going anywhere," he said.

As I left his room, two police officers went in. They were the same two who had arrived on the scene after Nick had been struck by the car.

. . .

Morgan sounded groggy when she said hello.

"Did I wake you up?" I said.

I heard silence at the other end of the line. Morgan was probably yawning. "I hear traffic," she said. "Where are you?"

"Downtown." I was outside the hospital, waiting for a bus back to my father's building so I could get the things Nick wanted.

"*Ohmygod*," she said.

"What's the matter?"

"What time is it, Robyn?"

"It's nearly three."

"Oh my god!"

"What's the matter, Morgan?"

"I'm late. I promised Billy." I heard what sounded like drawers opening and closing. "I can't even believe I agreed to this."

"Agreed to what?"

"I went down there with him two days ago. *And* this morning. I'm doing my best, Robyn. I love Billy, I really do. But this bird thing—"

"Agreed to what, Morgan?"

"I'm supposed to meet Billy at the DARC office. They're getting ready for the end-of-migration-season get-together tomorrow. Can you believe it? My whole Saturday has been devoted to dead birds, and he wants me to go to their wrap-up meeting too."

"Yeah, well, my day hasn't been much better. Nick and I went downtown—"

"You're spending the day with Nick and you're complaining?" Morgan said.

"I'm not exactly complaining. But he invited me to spend the day with him, and tomorrow we were supposed to go to the Santa Claus parade—"

"Oh," Morgan gasped. "I *love* parades! Do you think if I asked Billy, he'd ditch his meeting tomorrow and take me there?"

"Good luck," I said. To Billy, Santa was just a way to condition kids to think that happiness derived from material possessions—a concept that Billy rejected. Billy was flatly opposed to the rampant consumerism of the holiday season. He said the emphasis on acquiring more and more things contributed to a deteriorating environment. He felt the same way about the fashion industry, the fast-food industry, agribusiness, and the suburbs. It's hard to believe someone could have such strong opinions and still be such a nice guy.

"Maybe if I tell him that you and Nick are going?" Morgan said.

"We're not."

"But you just said—"

"Nick's in the hospital, Morgan. He got hit by a car."

"*What?* Is he okay?"

I told her what the doctor had said.

"Most people who get hit by cars aren't nearly that lucky," she said.

"There was a lot of traffic," I said, "so the car that hit him wasn't moving as fast as it could have been."

"Still, he'll probably have to kiss his job goodbye," Morgan said. "You know what those minimum-wage fast-food jobs are like. If you get sick or hurt, that's just too bad."

I hadn't thought about that. I wondered if Nick had. Unlike a lot of kids I knew, Nick didn't work because he wanted more spending money, or even because he was saving up for college. Nick worked to eat, keep a roof over his head, and buy the necessities. He *needed* a job.

"You want me to come down there and keep you company?" Morgan said. "I'm sure Billy would understand."

"Nice try," I said. "But didn't you promise Billy?" I spotted a bus lumbering toward me. "Gotta go, talk to you later." I tucked my phone back into my pocket and gulped the last of my coffee. As I dug in my purse for some money for bus fare, I thought again about my stolen backpack—with my bus pass inside of it.

. . .

All six of the apartments on the second floor of my father's building are more or less the same—living room, dining room, kitchen, bathroom, bedroom, all with high ceilings and plenty of windows. Nick had one of the apartments at the back of the building. He had been living there for a little over a month, but I had never been inside the place, so I was kind of curious when I unlocked the door.

The first thing that struck me when I stepped inside was how bare Nick's apartment was. My father had given him some old furniture he'd had stored in the basement—stuff from the apartment he'd lived in while the renovations were being done on the old carpet factory he'd inherited—but it looked like Nick hadn't added anything.

The second thing that struck me was how neat the place was. Which maybe wasn't that surprising, considering how few possessions Nick had. But the dishes had been washed and were sitting in a dish rack beside the sink. The table had been wiped clean. There was a stack of textbooks sitting in the middle of it and a stack of binders beside that. A planner lay open nearby. I glanced at it—Nick's homework assignments were all neatly recorded. I opened one of the binders. History. There was an essay inside. Nick had got a B-plus on it. I smiled.

Through the bedroom door I could see that he had made his bed and smoothed down the blankets. Maybe he'd gotten in the habit when he was at the group home. He had told me that they were pretty strict about neatness there. Everyone had chores too. Nick always complained that he pulled bathroom detail twice as often as anyone else. I peeked into his bathroom. Spotless. I smiled again, imagining him scrubbing every surface.

I went into the bedroom and opened the closet. Everything, including his jeans, was neatly hung up. I grabbed the pair with the widest legs so that he wouldn't have to cut the seam to get them to fit over his cast. While I was folding them, I glanced at a pile of papers on his bedside table. I moved a little closer. There were printed-out Craigslist job postings, a Help Wanted page torn from a local newspaper. Nick was looking for a job. Maybe a better one than he already had, one that paid more. Or maybe a second job.

I went back into the kitchen and got the plastic bag from the counter. I peeked inside—it contained a folded-up paper shopping bag with carrier handles and a pink woman's hat that I couldn't imagine Nick wearing. What did he want this stuff for? I put the jeans into the bag and headed back to the hospital.

. . .

The bed closest to the door in Nick's room was empty when I returned, and the curtain that divided the two beds was drawn all the way. I heard voices. Nick wasn't alone.

"I'll take care of it," he was saying. "Don't worry." There was a pause before he added, "You shouldn't even be here. What if someone saw you?"

"Mr. Chieu saw the accident," someone else said. A female voice. "He saw them take you in an ambulance. Someone had to come."

"What if you were followed?"

"I was careful. Besides, I'm just a clerk. I'm not anyone they would worry about."

"You should leave," Nick said. "I'll take care of things. Tell Mr. Li I promise."

"They want to know about what happened," the female voice said. "They want to know if it really was an accident or if someone saw what they were doing."

They? Who were they?

"You can tell them it was a stupid accident, that's all. You should really go, Sunny."

I stepped away from the door and ducked into the little waiting area down the hall. I stayed there for a few moments, out of sight. Finally I heard the same female voice say, "Be careful, Nick." I counted to ten and peeked out from the waiting area. A girl stood near the elevators. I recognized her immediately. She was the girl from the bakery—the girl that Nick had told me he didn't know. The elevator arrived and she stepped inside. When she turned to press the button for her floor, I ducked back out of sight and counted to ten again. Then I marched back to Nick's room and knocked on the open door.

"It's me," I called.

"Hey Robyn, come in."

Someone—Sunny?—had rolled his bed up for him. He still looked pale and I would have bet anything that he was in pain. But he managed a smile for me. He didn't get one in return.

"Guess who I just saw," I said.

He looked so wide-eyed and innocent, his purple eyes appearing darker than usual against the pallor of his skin.

"Who?"

"That girl from the bakery."

A surprised look appeared on his face. And a pretty good one. Anyone who didn't know Nick as well as I did might have been fooled by it.

"Here in the hospital?" he said.

I nodded.

"She must have been here visiting someone," Nick said. "It's a small world, huh?"

"An incredibly small world," I said. "I saw her at the elevator at the end of the hall just a minute ago."

Nick didn't say anything.

"And right before that, I saw her coming out of *this* room."

Still nothing.

"I heard you talking to her, Nick."

His pale face turned pink, then scarlet. "You were *spying* on me?"

"No. I was doing you a favor, remember? I went back to your place to get your stuff"—I threw the bag at him—"and when I got back here, I heard voices in your room. Yours and hers."

His eyes narrowed. "What did you hear?"

"Enough to know that you've been lying to me. You told me at the bakery that you didn't know that girl. But you do. What's going on, Nick? Who's Mr. Li? And what were you doing that would make him think that your getting hit by that car wasn't an accident? It has something to do with all that money. Doesn't it?"

He just stared at me.

"Fine," I said. Except that it wasn't fine at all. "Lie to me. Hide things from me. Pretend that everything is perfectly normal when it isn't. Do whatever you like, Nick. Get yourself into trouble again, if that's what you want. But you can do it alone. I'm out of here."

And I was. Out the door. Down the hall. Into the elevator. Out onto the street. Then, twenty minutes later, at Henri's place.

CHAPTER **EIGHT**

" Lemon?" Henri said.

"Sure," I said. "Please."

She squeezed a wedge of fresh lemon into a couple of mugs of tea and handed one of them to me. Then she sat down opposite me at the solid oak table that dominates the dining room of her old house. Henrietta Saint-Onge lives right in the heart of the city. Her closest neighbors—and they're so close that they're rubbing shoulders with her—are two office towers. They block out almost all of the sunlight that might otherwise travel into the house that has, for decades, miraculously avoided being torn down. Not that people—developers, politicians, the municipal government—haven't tried.

Henri's house stands smack in the middle of the financial district. The land it sits on is worth a small fortune. But Henri has turned down all offers. The house has been in her family for generations. She isn't interested in selling it to some developer who would flatten it and erect an office tower. She came close to losing it once, but she fought back. Henri knows a lot of people, and she mobilized all of them. The result: her house was declared a historic site—protected from demolition forever. She says that if she and Vern don't get around to getting married and having children, she's going to leave the house to the city to be turned into a museum after she dies.

"Mac dropped off your things," she said. "I put them in the back bedroom."

At the back of Henri's house, behind the living room, dining room, and kitchen, there are two smaller rooms. One is a guest bedroom that doubles as her office. It has an old-fashioned rolltop desk in it and an ultra-comfortable king-sized bed. It's where I always sleep when I stay at her house. The other is what Henri calls her den, where she keeps her TV. Henri's bedroom is a small room upstairs, just off the studio that occupies the rest of the second floor.

"Mac mentioned that you were spending the day with your boyfriend," she said. Henri had only met Nick once. She wrapped her hands around her mug and smiled expectantly at me from across the table.

"I don't know if you'd call him my boyfriend," I said.

"Oh?"

"I like him, and I think he likes me. But we're so different . . ."

"And?"

"And . . ." I stared down into my tea for a moment. "He doesn't tell me things. I always know when something is going on, but he doesn't always tell me what it is. Sometimes he shuts me out." *And sometimes he lies*, I thought, but I didn't want to admit that to Henri.

She looked closely at me. "It can be hard when you like somebody but you don't understand him," she said. "When I started going out with Vern, I could tell right away when he'd been assigned a bad case. I could read it on his face. But I could never get him to tell me about it." I knew exactly what she meant. My father had been the same way, according to my mother. It used to drive her crazy. It was also the number-one reason, my mother said, why cops had such a high divorce rate.

But this was different. What my father or Vern hadn't wanted to talk about were bad things that *other* people had done. But the things Nick didn't want to tell me about, well, I was pretty sure they were bad things that *he* was doing. But I couldn't tell Henri that.

"If you push too hard, they get mad and clam up tighter than ever," she said. "But if you back off and give them some space, they eventually learn they can trust you. I can't say that Vern tells me everything, because he doesn't. But he doesn't shut me out anymore the way he used to."

We had just finished our tea when my cell phone rang. I scrambled to answer it—I thought it might be Nick. It wasn't. It was Morgan.

"Are you back at the hospital?" she said.

"Nuh-uh. I'm at Henri's."

"So you aren't with Nick?"

"No. We had a fight."

"Thank goodness." Good old Morgan. Good old *sensitive* Morgan. "You have to get over here."

"Where are you?"

"Just down the street at the DARC office. You have to come down here right now, Robyn. You have to help me."

"Help you with what?"

Her voice dropped to a whisper. "Billy's coming," she said. "I can't tell you right now. I'll explain when you get here. Hurry, Robyn, okay?"

What a day.

"That was Morgan," I said to Henri after I put away my phone. "She needs me to help her with something."

"No problem," Henri said. She fished out a key from inside a chipped mug with a Picasso painting on it and tossed it to me. "I'm not going out," she said. "I have to keep moving on my project. But sometimes I get so caught up that I don't hear the doorbell. When you come back, just let yourself in."

I took the envelope of money out of my purse and stashed it under one of the pillows in the guest bedroom. Then I went to find out what Morgan's problem was.

.   .   .

Billy's mother is the head of public relations for one of the largest financial investment companies in the city. Billy had pestered her until she had finally arranged for him to make a presentation about DARC to some of the company's senior partners.

At the time, I told Billy he was probably wasting his breath. Why would people who were only interested in making money—which is how Billy always described them—care about little birds that crashed into their building? But Billy said it was worth a try: "You can't win if you don't play." And—why was I surprised?—he had been persuasive. The senior partners had turned out to be more warmhearted than I'd expected. Not only did they agree to shut off their office lights at night, they also made a donation to DARC and gave the organization some office space in one of the building's sub-basements. In the small office were a desk and computer, a cupboard full of equipment, and the chest freezer for storing dead birds.

The security guard at the main entrance to the office tower was sour-faced and stern when I pushed my way through a revolving door into the enormous, deserted lobby, but his face softened as soon as I mentioned DARC.

"You're looking for the bird boy," he said. He smiled as he shook his head. "Sometimes I think that kid is crazy, but he sure does care about those birds he finds."

That was Billy. Everybody who met him thought at first that he was slightly insane—an animal-loving, tree-hugging, fur-eschewing vegan idealist. But he always got to you. He cared so much, and knew so much about what he cared about, that he wore down almost everybody.

Even people who didn't agree with him ended up with grudging respect for him.

The security guard made me sign a visitors' log. Then I took the elevator down to the DARC office. Morgan was waiting for me when the doors opened.

"It's all my fault," she said. She was trying to keep her voice down, but she was so agitated that she didn't really succeed.

"What's wrong, Morgan?" I sniffed the air in the sub-basement. "And what's that smell?"

"I asked Billy about the Santa Claus parade." She paused. "Okay, so what actually happened was that I made a big deal about going to the parade. I said, 'I've been doing all the things you're interested in. When do we do the things I'm interested in?'" She glanced around and then grabbed me by the hand and pulled me away from the elevator. That was when I noticed that she was wearing disposable latex gloves.

"What's with the gloves? What's going on?"

"We had a fight," she said. "Billy actually got mad at me." She sounded stunned. "He called me materialistic."

"Oh." No surprise there. Morgan *is* materialistic. She loves to shop. In fact, I sometimes think she *lives* to shop. Morgan's idea of a great time is to score a great sweater or shoes at seventy-five percent off.

"He made me so angry that I—I called him naive."

"Ouch."

"And, well, we yelled at each other for a while and then, Robyn, I can't believe it, he told me he loved me."

"He did?" I couldn't help smiling. "And?"

"And—I can't believe this, either—I started to cry. Me!" Morgan is not the sentimental type. "Then do you know what he did? He made a bunch of phone calls. He rearranged the DARC meeting tomorrow. They're going to hold it later in the day. You know why?"

I had a pretty good idea, but I decided to humor her. "Why?"

"So that Billy can take me to the parade tomorrow." Her eyes started to glisten. "And so here we are."

"Where, exactly, are we? And why are you wearing those gloves?"

Morgan led me back in the direction we had just come, past the elevators and toward the hall outside the DARC office, where we found Billy and five other DARC members. I stared at them, trying to absorb what I was seeing.

Billy and the rest of DARC—most of whom were much older than Billy and all of whom were also wearing latex gloves—were hovering over a tarp spread across the floor. Nearby were two large bins. Billy and the others were reaching into the bins, pulling out plastic bags, and removing the contents. Each bag contained one or more birds. *Dead* birds. Well, that explained the smell.

"Hey, Robyn," Billy said. He had been sitting cross-legged on the floor beside one of the bins, but he stood up as soon as he saw me. He was holding a plastic bag in one hand. "Morgan told me what happened. How's Nick?"

"Well, actually . . ." I began. I would have kept going, but Morgan pinched the back of my arm—*hard*—a signal for me to shut up. It was also a signal for me to pinch her back just as hard at my earliest convenience.

"Robyn's really upset, Billy," she said.

"Well, then, why don't you stick around?" Billy said. "You can help us. It'll take your mind off things." While he talked, he opened the ziplock bag he was holding, reached in, and pulled out a dead bird with a yellow belly. It looked so tiny in the palm of his hand. "Kentucky warbler," he said. "We picked up a lot of warblers this year." He held it out to me so I could get a closer look—and an even closer smell. "Grab some gloves. There's a box of them over there."

"Robyn wants to talk to me, Billy," Morgan said. "We'll be back in a few minutes, okay?"

"Is there anything I can do?" Billy said. His do-gooder eyes were filled with concern.

Before I could answer, Morgan grabbed me by the hand and dragged me away from the tarp and bins and dead birds in plastic baggies. We were out of sight of the DARC people before I remembered what she was wearing. I stared down at her disposable gloves.

"You better not have touched something dead with those," I said.

Morgan looked at her hands. Her mouth formed a great big O. She yanked her hands away from me and stripped off the gloves.

"*Eeew!*" I said. "Thanks a lot!"

"There's a bathroom just down here." She led me through a narrow corridor and pushed open a door. I raced to the bank of sinks inside and washed my hands under the hottest water I could stand.

"They're taking all of the birds out of the bags and classifying them," she said. "Sparrows in one place, warblers in another, thrushes in this pile, hummingbirds in that, jays, ovenbirds, woodcocks, juncos . . ." I was impressed by the number of species she could name. "They're going to arrange them on a white background and take a picture. It's supposed to give everyone an instant idea of how many birds get killed every season, why more buildings should shut off their lights at night. You know, visual impact. Billy thinks he can use it to get some funding for DARC. He wants to get more people involved."

"Sounds like a good plan," I said. "What's the problem?"

"You saw what Billy had in his hand." she said. "I actually touched some of them." She gave me an agonized look. "The first one I pulled out of the freezer was a woodcock. Big. Ugly. Long, skinny beak. And this one's eyes were open. I was holding it in my hand and, I don't know, it gave me the creeps. I started shaking all over. I don't like dead things, Robyn. So then I thought, okay, maybe the smaller birds would be less creepy."

The look of horror on her face told me that she had discovered otherwise. "But the smaller they are, the faster they thaw out. And when they thaw, they start to smell. After a while it gets to you. I've spent the past half hour trying not to throw up. Then there was this one bird—it looked like it had been partly eaten by bugs or something. I had to run to the bathroom. Now I don't know what to do. I can't touch another one of those things. But if I don't go back, Billy's going to be disappointed in me."

Morgan isn't normally the kind of person who worries about what other people think of her. She sees herself as above that. Above everything and everyone, in fact. If you consider yourself better and smarter than everyone else, why worry about what they're thinking? But apparently Morgan cared what Billy thought of her.

"Some people faint at the sight of blood," I said. "Some can't handle heights. It's no big deal. Just tell him the truth."

"I can't," she said. "I just can't."

"Morgan, you either have to tell him the truth or you have to hold your breath, fight back the nausea, and touch more dead birds. You have no other choice."

She looked down at her feet. *Here it comes*, I thought. *She has a plan, and it involves me.*

"Thing is, Robyn, I told Billy that you called me."

"But *you* called *me*."

She looked up at me. "I know. But that's not what I told Billy. I told him that you called me and that you were crying hysterically—"

"Hysterically?"

"Well—"

"*Hysterically*, Morgan?"

At least she had the decency to look embarrassed. "I'm sorry," she said. "But I couldn't tell him the truth. I love him. I don't want him to think I'm a wuss."

"There's nothing like an open and honest relationship."

"Billy founded DARC. He believes in it one hundred percent. He thinks it's making a difference. It *is* making a difference. Some of the office buildings down here are actually trying to keep most of their lights off at night. I can't tell him that the thing he's most proud of makes me want to throw up."

"And your solution is?"

"I was going to tell him that you need someone to talk to right now. You know, girl talk. Billy will understand."

"You realize that he'll be *understanding* a lie, right?"

"I have to get out of here, Robyn. I'd do the same for you."

I knew she would. Morgan could be self-centered. She could also be annoyingly superior. But she was also a loyal friend.

"Okay," I said. "But you owe me."

Morgan turned out to be right. Billy said he understood how I felt, that it must have been awful to see Nick actually get hit by a car. He said that Nick had been incredibly lucky and that he was going to be just fine. Then he pulled Morgan aside. He was still wearing his rubber gloves. Morgan cringed, but she managed to hide most of her revulsion. Billy said something to her in a soft voice. Then he kissed her.

Suddenly Morgan didn't seem to care about the gloves. In fact, I don't think that she would have cared if Billy were covered head to toe in dead bird residue. She wrapped her arms around him. I thought they were never going to come up for air. Some of the other DARC members glanced at them. A middle-aged man with a salt-and-pepper beard smiled wistfully. Finally they parted, and Billy said he would call Morgan later. As we got into the elevator, Morgan wiped a tear from her eye.

"Do you know what he said?" she said. "Billy said I was the nicest, most considerate person he knew and that you're lucky to have me as a friend."

"Uh-huh." Either Billy had been experiencing a completely different Morgan from the rest of the world over the past ten or so years, or love really was blind.

We signed out at the security desk and stepped out onto the sidewalk.

"So now that you're sprung, what are you going to do?" I said.

"Go home, take a nice long bubble bath, and crawl back into bed," she said. "You?"

"Go back to Henri's, I guess."

"What about Nick?"

"What about him?"

She looked at me. "You weren't kidding, were you? You two really had a fight."

"A big one," I said.

Morgan hooked an arm through mine. "Come on," she said. "Let's go for coffee. You can tell me all about it."

We were on our way to Morgan's favorite coffee shop when I heard someone call my name.

"Uh-oh," Morgan said. "It's Barry."

Barry Osler—life objective: millionaire by age thirty—was beefier than the burgers he served up in his restaurant and had a complexion that was oilier than his fry pit.

"Maybe he wants to ask you out again," Morgan said.

"Let's pretend we didn't see him," I said.

"Too late," Morgan said.

Barry was scurrying toward us, his jacket flapping open over his fast-food uniform and his name badge—*Barry. Manager*.

"Robyn," he said, beaming and breathless. "What a coincidence. I was thinking about you. I was going to call you."

"I told you so," Morgan whispered.

"Hi Barry," I said. "How are you?"

Most people recognize that question for what it is—a polite but empty greeting. Barry was not one of those people. He shook his head and sighed. "That's exactly why I was going to call you. When I tell people that I'm a manager at a restaurant, they think, how hard could that be? But it's way harder than it looks. You know why?" He didn't pause to let me even attempt an answer. "It's true what they say—good help really *is* hard to find. Just last week, one of my employees stopped coming in for his shift. Just like that. When I called him to find out where he was, he said, 'Oh yeah, I forgot to tell you. I quit.' Like he wouldn't have let me know if I hadn't tracked him down. The same week I had to fire another guy. I can't tell you the trouble *he* caused. That's when I thought of you, Robyn. You'd be a great addition to my team. Christmas is just around the corner. Who couldn't use some extra money, am I right?"

Morgan nudged me. I elbowed her back—hard.

"Thanks for thinking of me," I said. "But I'm pretty swamped with school right now."

"Actually," Morgan said, "I think Robyn's boyfriend works at your place. Isn't that what you told me, Robyn?"

Barry looked confused. "Boyfriend?" He stared at me as if he were my boyfriend—and he'd just discovered that I was cheating on him.

"Nick D'Angelo," Morgan said, oh-so-sweetly. She was going to be sorry if Barry decided to make things hard for Nick. "He works for you, right?"

"That guy is your *boyfriend?*" Barry said. "I never thought you'd associate with someone like that."

"Excuse me?"

"Nick is the guy I fired last week—after some friends of his came in and busted up the place for the *second* time. I had to call the cops." He seemed to enjoy breaking this particular bit of news. "That guy was nothing but trouble. Always giving me attitude. I hope he isn't expecting a reference from me, because he isn't going to get one." He dug a business card out of his pocket and handed it to me. "Any time you want a job, give me a call. I know you'd be a model employee."

"So much for that romance," Morgan said after he had left. "Barry won't bother you again, which I think makes us even. How come you didn't tell me that Nick got fired?" Morgan likes to think of herself as smart. As in straight As all the way. Proof that she's as smart as she thinks she is: all it took was a glance at the expression on my face before she said, "Ah."

We went into the coffee shop and ordered lattes, even though I didn't want one anymore. I didn't want anything. Morgan insisted.

"It'll cheer you up," she said. Lattes are her second-favorite pick-me-up, after shopping. While we sipped our coffee, Morgan said that she was sure Nick had been planning to tell me he'd been fired. She said he was probably embarrassed by what had happened. I wasn't so sure, and was about to say so when her phone rang. It was Billy. Morgan was perky by the time she hung up.

"Billy says he hopes you're feeling better," she said.

"Actually, I'm feeling worse. But you can tell him thanks for asking."

"They've finished sorting birds. Billy wants me to meet him. We're going over to his place. He wants to know if you want to come."

I said no and tried not to notice how relieved she seemed. She wanted alone time with Billy. I understood. When Nick had called me last night, that was exactly what *I* had wanted. But that was then.

We finished our lattes—Morgan chugged hers down like water—and skipped off to meet Billy. I trudged back to Henri's place.

"Robyn, is that you?" Henri called when I unlocked the door and pushed it open. When I called back that it was, she said, "You've got company."

I found Henri standing in the kitchen, pouring boiling water into a mug. Sitting at Henri's kitchen table, his cast resting on a pillow that Henri had put on one of the chairs, was Nick.

CHAPTER **NINE**

"Hey, Robyn," Nick said. He looked at me, searching for a sign that I wasn't still mad at him.

Henri put a steaming mug of tea in front of Nick and asked me if I'd like some. When I said no, thanks, she said, "Well, I'd better get back to work. I'll be upstairs if anyone needs me."

Nick watched her go. "She's nice," he said.

"I thought they wanted to keep you in the hospital overnight," I said, unbuttoning my jacket.

"I guess they changed their minds," he said.

"You guess? What did the doctor say when he discharged you?"

He just shrugged.

"You talked to the doctor before you left the hospital, right?"

"It's no big deal, Robyn," he said. Terrific. He'd been lying to me all day. He'd been doing something that was probably illegal. He'd been hit by a car. And now he was deciding to play doctor. I stopped unbuttoning my coat and started buttoning it again. I grabbed my gloves and headed for the door.

"Hey," Nick said. "Don't go."

I heard him groan and turned to find him white-faced as he struggled onto his good foot. The chair he was clinging to for balance teetered. For a moment I thought it was going to topple over. But I didn't rush to help him.

"Did you talk to the doctor before you left the hospital?" I said again.

He grimaced. Maybe he was angry. He had to be in pain. But he didn't answer. I turned for the door again.

"Okay," he said. "God, sometimes you act so much like your mom it's scary."

"Are you trying to charm me, Nick? If you are, it's not working."

"They didn't discharge me. I just sort of walked out."

"Sort of?"

"Well, I hobbled. These crutches are murder." He grinned. He *was* trying to charm me.

"Does your aunt know where you are? If she goes to the hospital to see you and you aren't there—"

"What's with you?" he said. "I called her, okay?"

"What did she say?"

"Nothing."

"Right." I tried to tell myself that I didn't care, but the truth was I was getting angrier and angrier.

"I left a message," Nick said. "Give me a break, Robyn. I came all the way over here to see you."

"What for? To tell me more lies?" Then it hit me. "You want the money," I said. I went into the back bedroom, grabbed the thick envelope from where I had stashed it, marched back into the kitchen, and threw it at him.

"Hey!" Nick said, his own anger flashing. "You want to at least *try* to be nice to me? I got hit by a car, remember?"

"You told me you had the weekend off, Nick."

I was giving him the perfect chance to do what Morgan had been so sure he would do—tell me the truth about losing his job. Instead, he looked down at the floor and didn't say a word.

"I spoke to Barry," I said. "Barry, your boss."

He looked up at me, surprised.

"What were you doing? Checking up on me?" he said.

"I ran into him. I know him, Nick. He goes to my school."

"Yeah, well, he's a jerk."

"He thinks just as highly of you," I said. "He told me he fired you last week."

"So what? It was a lousy job."

"He said some of your friends trashed the place. Twice."

"They weren't friends of mine."

"Whatever." I couldn't tell anymore whether he was lying or telling the truth. "You got fired and you didn't tell me."

"You're not my mom, Robyn," he said. He sounded as angry as I was. "You're not my youth worker, either. Since when do I have to tell you every detail of my life?"

"Since never, I guess."

He winced as he tried to maneuver around the chair so that he could sit down again. This time the chair started to tip. I rushed forward to right it. Nick grabbed me around the waist for balance. We stood there for a moment, Nick clinging to me, me wanting to break free of him but feeling trapped by the heat of his body. I helped him sit down. His face shone with perspiration. He took a deep breath before lifting his injured foot back onto the pillow. The jagged scar across his face stood out against his pale skin, and for some reason that got to me. I felt sorry for him.

"Didn't they give you anything for pain?" I said.

"They were going to. But I left before the nurse came back."

"You want me to see if Henri has anything?"

He started to shake his head, then drew in a sharp breath and closed his eyes, breathing hard through the pain.

"Yeah," he said. "Maybe."

I went to find Henri, who gave me a bottle of medium-strength pain relievers from her medicine cabinet. Nick took two of them. Then he patted the seat of the chair next to his. I hesitated. Theoretically, I was still angry with him.

"Please?" he said. There were those purple eyes of his, begging me. What could I do? I sat down. "I didn't tell you about getting fired because I didn't want you to worry," he said. "Besides, I thought if I could get another job first, it wouldn't be a big deal."

"Because then you could tell me you quit the first job, right?"

Some color returned to his cheeks—the bright red of embarrassment.

"Something like that," he said. "I'm sorry, okay?"

My mother used to say that the two things that drove her crazy about my father were when he didn't apologize, and when he did. (Actually, there were a lot more things about him that drove her crazy, which is why they got divorced.) When he was a cop, my dad worked long hours. He missed a lot of occasions that my mother thought he shouldn't have. Half the time, she said, he refused to apologize. "It's my job," he'd say. "You want me to apologize because some piece of garbage decided to kill his girlfriend, and I had to go and find him? That's supposed to be my fault?" She hated when he did that—what could she say?

The rest of the time, he would say, "I apologize. I know that [fill-in-the-blank occasion] was important to you and I'm sorry I missed it." She hated that because she knew he wasn't even remotely sorry that he had missed whatever it was; he was only sorry that she was upset, and that if he didn't apologize, she would go on and on about it. According to my mother, that didn't constitute a real apology. A real apology, she said, was when someone regretted what they had done, understood why it was wrong, and tried never to do it again, which, of course, my father never did.

I looked at Nick. I thought about how many times he had said sorry to me. I wondered what he was thinking when he said it.

"So what are you going to do?" I said.

"I don't know. They said at the hospital that I have to be on crutches for six weeks. My ankle's too busted up for a walking cast. Who's going to hire me when I can't even walk? What am I gonna do if I can't get a job?"

"You could talk to your aunt."

He shook his head. "Talking to my aunt means begging Glen. Not a chance."

"Then you'll have to talk to my dad. I know he doesn't care about the rent. And I could lend you some money for food and—"

"No way." He sounded angry again. "I'm not asking your dad for anything. And I'm not taking money from you."

I could have argued with him, but what would have been the point? Besides, it was still two weeks until his rent would be due and he would have other bills to pay. Maybe something would happen by then. Maybe a miracle. We sat together in silence for a few moments. Then I couldn't stand it anymore.

"Nick, what's going on with you?"

"You mean about getting fired?"

"That. And the bruise on your neck. And the way you and that cop looked at each other this morning. And the girl from the bakery who turned up at the hospital. And the envelope full of money. And the guy who pushed you. What did the cops say when you told them about him?"

He looked down at the floor again.

"You didn't tell them?" I couldn't believe it. I started to stand. He grabbed my hand and pulled me back down.

"I told you, Robyn. That was an accident."

"Really?" I said. I pictured the tall, blond guy smiling down at Nick's limp body lying on the road. "And when that girl from the bakery who you didn't know came to the hospital? Was that was an accident too?" I yanked my hand away.

"Come on, Robyn."

"Don't lie to me, Nick."

He studied me for a moment. "It's complicated."

"I'm on the honor roll. I think I can handle complicated."

He took both of my hands in his, held tight, and peered deep into my eyes. He looked more serious than I had ever seen him.

"I need your help," he said. "I need you to do something for me."

I waited.

"Before I tell you what it is, you have to promise me that, no matter what, you won't tell anyone."

I hesitated. I liked Nick. Truthfully, I was pretty sure I loved him. And if you love someone, you'll do anything for them, right?

He tugged gently on my hands to make me look at him. "Robyn? Promise?"

"I promise," I said. And then I held my breath.

He glanced around. Then he struggled to his feet and worked his crutches under his arms.

"Where are you—?"

He held a finger to his lips. I watched as he struggled toward the door that led to the foyer and the stairs. He listened for a moment. I could hear Henri moving around upstairs and faint strains of music from her speakers. When Henri works, she always listens to music—usually the same piece of music over and over. Nick closed the door. He tried a turn on his crutches and almost lost his balance. Pain flashed in his eyes, but he righted himself and hobbled back to the table.

"I need you to deliver the money for me," he said.

"*What?*" I must have said it louder than I'd intended because Nick glanced nervously at the closed door. I dropped my voice. "You mean the money you collected this morning?"

He nodded. "It has to be delivered. My ankle is killing me, Robyn. I don't think I've ever hurt so much in my life. Will you help me out? Will you deliver it?"

"To who? And why?"

"All you have to do is go to the parade tomorrow and hand it to a guy."

"What's the money *for?*"

"That's not important."

"Who's the guy?"

"That's not important, either."

"What's in the other envelope?"

"What other envelope?"

"There's a sealed envelope in with the money." Whatever was in it was stiff and squarish. "What's in it?"

"I don't know."

I gave him a look.

"I swear it, Robyn. I don't know."

I was getting a bad feeling. "Is it illegal, Nick?"

I hoped he would say no. I expected him to give me an evasive answer. But what he actually said was, "I don't know."

"You don't know?"

"I didn't ask."

"You spent the whole day collecting money, which you've agreed to deliver to *a guy*, and you don't even know if what you're doing is illegal?"

"I'm doing it as a favor."

"Like the favor you were going to do for Joey?" Nick had tried to cover for his stepbrother Joey back in the summer. If the truth hadn't come out, Nick would have been locked up and Joey would have been free.

Nick fixed me with his eyes. "Okay," he said. "I'll tell you. One night, a couple of years ago, I was out late. Later than I should have been. On account of Duane." Duane. Joey's father, Nick's stepfather. The guy who had put the scar on Nick's face and made him an orphan. "And there were these guys. Tough guys. At least, they thought they were. And I was just a kid.

"They started in on me, you know? It was right downtown, but the streets were deserted. They gave me the line, 'Your money or your life.' At first I thought they were kidding. But they weren't. I think they were on something, at least a couple of them. They started shoving. Then one hit me. The next thing I know I'm on the ground and these guys are kicking me. I thought I was going to die. I really did."

I stared at him. I'd known him for a couple of months now, but he kept surprising me with things I didn't know, things I never could have imagined.

"And then, out of nowhere, there's this other guy. He's yelling at them. He's holding up a cell phone and telling them, 'I called the cops; the cops are on their way.' And, I don't know, like I said, I think at least some of them were on something. They rush this guy and they start stomping him. They were really going on him. Then I saw lights and heard the cop cars coming. I'm not sure what happened next. I woke up in the hospital. My mother was there, crying. Joey too." He tugged on his T-shirt, yanked it free of his belt and halfway up his back. He bent over. "See that?" he said.

There were two marks on his back, faded, but you could tell they had been deep when they were made.

"A guy with steel-toed boots did that to me. Broke three ribs. I was in the hospital for two weeks, at home for a month after that, with Duane the whole time acting like I was faking it."

"What happened to the guy who helped you?" I said.

"He was a pizza delivery guy. Nineteen years old." He shook his head. "He didn't make it."

"Oh."

"You know the restaurant where we had lunch today? The cook there is the guy's father. He came to see me in the hospital that time. We stayed in touch. I told him, 'If there's ever anything I can do, all you have to do is ask. Anything.'" He looked down at the envelope. "Yesterday he asked. And I said yes. I didn't ask any questions. I owe him, Robyn. So what do you say? Will you help?"

I could understand why Nick felt a debt to this man. I could even understand why he agreed to deliver a lot of money to a mystery person at the Santa Claus parade. But was that a good enough reason for me to do something that didn't feel right?

"No," I said.

"Come on, Robyn. I wouldn't ask if I didn't have to. But I can't do it myself. I can barely walk."

He had been collecting money all day. I don't know how much it totaled, but it was a lot. So much cash, so much secrecy—it had to mean trouble.

"No," I said again.

He slammed his fist down onto the table. "I knew I shouldn't have gotten you involved. I knew you would freak out if you found out about the money. You're so suspicious all the time. I should have asked Beej!"

Beej was a surly, spiky-haired girl with no fixed address. She was also a friend of Nick's, but her view of the world was even more cynical than his.

"So why didn't you?" I said, as angry as he was.

"Because I couldn't get in touch with her."

"You mean, you tried?"

He didn't answer.

I thought about what he had just said: that he shouldn't have gotten me involved.

"You wanted someone with you today while you collected that money, didn't you?" I said. He didn't answer, but I saw a flicker of something in his eyes. "Why?" I said.

Still no answer.

What had the girl from the bakery asked? If Nick's accident really was an accident, or if someone had seen what he'd been doing?

"Was someone watching us today, Nick?" I said.

Nothing.

"The man who sent you to collect that money—he was worried you might be watched, right?" I said. I shook my head. That couldn't be it. If Nick had been worried that he was being watched, what good would it do him to drag me along? I thought back to what the girl had said in the hospital—"they want to know if it really was an accident, or if someone saw what they were doing." What *they* were doing, not what Nick was doing.

"You're not the one who was afraid of being watched," I said. "It was the people you were collecting money from. *They* were afraid someone would see." But afraid of who? "They didn't want anyone to know they were giving you money, is that it? That's why you wanted me there—so we would look like a regular couple out shopping together. It's not like we're part of the community. It's not like anyone would think those people would hand money over to a couple of kids. Is that it?" It was the only thing that made sense. It also explained what he had said about Beej. "If you could have gotten in touch with Beej, you would have taken *her* with you, right?" He wouldn't even look at me, which told me what I needed to know. "Great. So, basically, I'm second string. You tried Beej first because you knew she wouldn't ask any questions. But you couldn't track her down." Still nothing. "I haven't heard from you in ages. I thought you missed me. I thought you really wanted to see me. But you only called me because you couldn't get hold of Beej. Thanks a lot, Nick."

Finally Nick raised his head. His eyes flashed with anger. "No. Thank *you*, Robyn. I need someone to help me out. And what do you do? You refuse. You keep telling me you care. You've got a funny way of showing it."

We glared at each other, each of us mad for a different reason. I told myself there was nothing he could do to change my mind. Then: "I love you, Robyn, but I don't get you."

"What?"

"I don't understand you. You live in this world where everything is perfect, where you never have to worry about what's going to happen tomorrow. You have this perfect mom and this perfect dad and they'd anything to make sure you're okay. But it's not like that in my world."

Fine, except that I was still stuck on those three little words. "You said something else," I said.

He gave me a blank look.

"Before you said you didn't get me. You said . . ." Maybe he hadn't meant it. Maybe it was just a throwaway line.

"I love you," he said. Again. He took my hand. "I know you care about me, Robyn, even if I drive you crazy sometimes. I care about you too. But right now I need your help." I looked deep into his eyes and saw a different Nick than the one the rest of the world saw. I didn't see the scar. I didn't see the long list of run-ins with the police. I didn't see the twelve months spent in custody. I didn't even see the lies. I just saw the Nick who said he loved me, the Nick I was pretty sure I loved back. The Nick who was perilously close to getting himself into deep trouble—there was no doubt in my mind.

"Okay," I said. "I'll do it."

CHAPTER **TEN**

It was a lie. I had looked right into Nick's eyes and I had flat-out lied. But from the relief on his face, I could tell he believed me. He gripped my hand and pulled me closer to him so that he could kiss me. I felt bad about that—he was kissing me because I had made a promise I had no intention of keeping. But I let him kiss me anyway. I told myself that I had lied for his own good, to protect him, to stop him from getting into trouble again.

"What exactly do I have to do?" I said, as soon as I could catch my breath.

"Practically nothing," he said. "It's totally safe. I wouldn't ask you if it wasn't." All I had to do was show up at the Santa Claus parade at noon the next day, along with tens of thousands of other people. I didn't have to stand in any particular location—"Just stay on the east side of the street," he said, "somewhere in the middle of the crowd. You'll blend in that way."

"How do I know who to give it to?"

"You don't have to worry about that. The person will find you. Can you grab the bag that's with my coat in the front hall?"

I retrieved the bag that I had brought from his apartment and handed it to him. He pulled out the pink hat and the folded-up paper shopping bag from a bookstore chain. Someone had stuck a big Christmas tree sticker over the store logo on one side of it.

"You wear this," he said, holding up the hat. "And carry this." The shopping bag. "The money will be in the bag." He picked up the envelope I had thrown at him and dropped it in. "Someone will take it from you. That's it."

"And you really don't know what this is all about?" I said.

He shook his head. "But I trust Mr. Li. And I owe him big. It'll be easy, Robyn. You'll see."

I took the bag and the hat from him and started toward the back of the house.

"Where are you going?" Nick said.

"To put this away."

.   .   .

Henri came down from her studio and asked if we were hungry. I glanced at my watch. It was late. Neither of us had eaten since lunch.

"I was thinking of ordering pizza," Henri said. "Are you guys interested?"

"Definitely," I said.

When the food arrived, we took it into Henri's den and Henri popped a movie into her DVD player. Halfway through, she nudged me and nodded at Nick. He had fallen asleep on the couch beside me.

"He had a rough day," I said.

"It's not every day you get hit by a car," Henri agreed.

We decided to let him sleep. When the movie was over, Henri said, "Should we call someone?"

I told her that there was no one to call. "He lives alone. His aunt knows where he is."

"Well, in that case," Henri said, "I guess I'd better find some sheets."

She was back a few minutes later with a couple of pillows and two heavy wool blankets. Nick woke up long enough for Henri to check that he wasn't suffering from the effects of a concussion. Then we tucked him in and left the room. As Henri pulled the door shut, she said, "Be good, Robyn."

. . .

As I got ready for bed, I stared at the shopping bag with the money in it. Now that I had it, what was I going to do with it? I lay back on the bed and tried to decide if I should call my father. But what would I tell him? That Nick was up to something that might or might not be illegal? Who was I kidding? What type of legal activity could possibly involve surreptitiously collecting money—a *lot* of money—from people and then handing it over to a mysterious, unknown party? If I told my father about it, what would he do—besides forbid me to deliver the cash? He would say it didn't smell right. And then he would want to alert the police. And what would *they* do? Put Nick under surveillance? Question him? Knowing Nick, he wouldn't cooperate, not if it meant breaking a promise. So he would get in trouble. Again. And Nick couldn't afford any more trouble. Not with his record. Not when he was trying so hard. He was in school. He was working—well, he *had* been working. But I believed he was trying. I really did. If there was any way that I could make sure that he and trouble didn't have a head-on collision, then I'd do it. But how? And what was I going to do about the money? Or that sealed envelope?

I tiptoed to the door and peeked out. All the lights were out on the ground floor. Henri had gone upstairs and Nick was asleep in the den. I closed the door, picked up the bookstore bag, and tipped it out onto the bed. Out slid the bright pink hat and the thick envelope, folded and held shut with rubber bands. I slipped off the bands and opened it up. Inside, with the money, was the smaller, sealed envelope, the one that had felt different.

I crept over to Henri's rolltop desk. I felt like a criminal as searched the drawers. Finally I found what I was looking for—a box of plain white envelopes. I pulled one out and held it next to the sealed envelope. It was exactly the same size. Nick would never know the difference.

I ripped open the seal and spent the next few minutes staring at what was inside.

The envelope contained two documents: a passport for a girl I had never seen before and a visa for entry into the United States. Why were they in with the money? Who was Nick delivering them to, and why? I could think of only one explanation. It wasn't even remotely legal.

I glanced at the clock on the bedside table. It was almost midnight. I had been up for twenty hours. Nick had said that I had to be at the parade at noon. I put the money, the documents, and the hat back into the bag and set it at the foot of the bed. Then I set the clock's alarm for eight. I planned to get up early, think things through, and decide what to do—after I'd had a good night's sleep. I told myself I had plenty of time.

. . .

I was dressed like a Swiss Miss. My mid-length curly hair had miraculously grown long enough to be braided into two thick plaits. I was in the mountains—the Alps, I think—watching dozens of little clouds that dotted the mountainside. No, wait. Not clouds. They were sheep. Bleating sheep. The sound coming from those sweet, fluffy creatures was surprisingly annoying.

I rolled over and opened one eye.

I wasn't in the mountains after all. I was in Henri's spare bedroom. And the bleating was coming from the alarm clock. I squinted at it. My other eye popped open. I grabbed the clock and bolted upright.

Eleven o'clock. I had set the alarm for eight and it was now eleven!

I threw back the covers and raced out of the room. The door to the den was closed. I relaxed a little. Nick was still in bed. He had probably been as exhausted as I was. I hustled to the kitchen in sock feet and checked the clock over the stove. Yup, it really was eleven o'clock.

I heard the front door open and close again. Henri appeared and set a plastic shopping bag down on the table. She shrugged out of her coat.

"It's really chilly out there," she said. "But sunny. I went down to the waterfront and took a long walk. Nothing like a good stroll to get the creative juices flowing." She held up the bag. "I've got bagels. They were still warm when I bought them. Want one?"

I glanced back at the door to the study. "I should probably wake Nick."

Henri laughed. "He was up when I got up. He looked a lot better than he did last night. I fed him before I went out. That boy has a *big* appetite. He was sitting here reading the newspaper when I left." She nodded at the Sunday paper, which was spread out on the table. I glanced at it—and gasped. "Is something wrong?" Henri said.

The paper was open to the Metro section. I picked it up. The lead story was about a shooting the previous night in Chinatown. There was a picture of the victim beside the article. I recognized him even without reading the name printed underneath. It was the cook from the restaurant where Nick and I had had lunch yesterday. Mr. Li, the man Nick owed a favor to. He had been shot dead in the alley behind the restaurant.

I ran to the den and shoved open the door.

"Robyn," Henri called after me. "Are you okay?"

Two pillows sat one on top of the other at one end of the sofa. Next to them were two neatly folded blankets. Nick was gone.

I ran to Henri's guest room.

I had left the bag with the money at the foot of the bed. It wasn't there anymore. Nick must have taken it. But why? I had said I would deliver it for him. Hadn't he believed me? I glanced at the clock. I was sure I'd set the alarm for eight, but when I checked it, it was set for eleven.

I dressed quickly and went back out into the kitchen.

"What time did Nick get up?" I said.

"I came down at seven and he was already awake."

"What time did you go out?"

"Maybe half an hour later. Why?"

Nick had gotten up early. He must have seen the article in the paper. And snuck into my room, taken the money, and reset the alarm. I headed for the door and pulled on my jacket and scarf.

"What's the matter, Robyn?" Henri said. "Where are you going?"

"To the parade," I said as I opened the door. "To find Nick."

· · ·

By the time I reached the parade route, it was almost noon and the streets were jammed. The people who had arrived the earliest, right up front, came prepared with folding chairs, blankets, Thermoses of hot cocoa or coffee. Behind them, filling the sidewalks, were the latecomers. The smaller children were in front, peeping out between the heads and shoulders of the seated parade-watchers. The parents were in back.

As I headed up the east side of the street. I heard what sounded like dozens of snare drums and bass drums in the distance, followed by the blast of trumpets and horns, tubas and trombones. The parade had started and was working its way toward where I was standing. I wove my way through the crowd, searching for a bright pink hat. Stay on the east side of the street, Nick had said, and the mystery person will find you. But there were thousands of people on the sidewalk. They wore hats, mitts, scarves, and jackets of every conceivable color.

The first band marched into sight, blaring festive music. A dozen or so clowns fanned out ahead of it, running up to kids at the front of the crowd and handing out miniature candy canes. I kept moving, twisting this way and that, scanning the crowd. If Nick was here, he would have staked out a place and would probably stay put until he was relieved of the money. He would have to. There was no way he could move easily through this crowd on crutches. Still, trying to find him was like trying to find one teeny light on a giant Christmas tree.

Then I spotted it—a flash of bright pink.

Spotted it and lost it. The crowd closed in around me as I waded toward where I thought I'd seen the hat. I glimpsed it again, for a split second, and then, like a firefly on a July night, it vanished. I pressed forward, scanning heads and—yes!—there was Nick, looking both serious and silly as he peered around in the bright pink hat. He was standing at the outer edge of the crowd, off the sidewalk and on the lawn in front of a hospital. People swirled around him, some trying to squeeze into the front ranks of the parade watchers, others moving to circumvent the festivities by cutting across the hospital property. Except for the hat, Nick was dressed completely in black. He leaned heavily on his crutches. The paper bookstore bag with the Christmas tree sticker dangled from one hand. His face was pale, despite the chill in the air, and I guessed he must be in pain.

I opened my mouth to call to him but then decided against it. I pushed through the throng until I finally reached him. When I touched his shoulder, he jumped and twisted around.

"Robyn." He did not look pleased to see me. "What are you doing here?"

"You asked me to be here, remember?" I said.

"I changed my mind. I can handle this myself."

"What about your ankle? Doesn't it hurt?"

"It's fine."

"I saw the newspaper, Nick. I know the old man you were talking to yesterday is dead. I saw his picture."

"You should leave, Robyn. Now."

"I also know what's in the envelope. And it's not money."

His expression was completely blank. How naive could a person be? I had learned my lesson about sealed envelopes thanks to Trisha Carnegie's stepfather, but it looked like Nick hadn't. He had agreed to do a favor for someone he trusted. He hadn't asked any questions. And it had never occurred to him to look in the envelope.

"It's a passport and a visa, Nick. You know what that means, don't you?"

Nothing. Not a word.

"You heard about those illegal immigrants, right? The ones they found in that shipping container down at the docks? What about the Chinese man who was shot a couple of days ago? The police think he had something to do with the immigrants. The people who bring illegals into the country charge them a lot of money. The smugglers get them forged IDs—like passports and visas."

I could tell by the way he was staring past me that he wasn't listening. If he were six instead of sixteen, he probably would have jammed his fingers into his ears and started humming to block out my voice completely.

"Nick, if you were smart—"

"Right," he said, giving the word a bitter flavor. "*If* I were smart. Obviously I'm not—not compared to you, right? I don't mess with your life, Robyn. How about you don't mess with mine either."

"But if this involves illegal immigrants—"

"Do me a favor, Robyn. For once don't give me one of your big lectures about how you're right and I'm wrong. Just get lost, okay?"

"Come on, Nick. Think about it."

"Get out of here."

I stayed put.

"Look, Robyn, I know you said you'd help me. But you and I both know you were never going to do it." I tried to look indignant, but it was hard because he was right. "You were probably going to call your mom or your dad. On top of that," he said, "the envelope was sealed, but you opened it. So don't look all hurt and innocent, like you're some little angel and I'm the one who's doing something wrong, okay? Just get out of here and let me do what I have to do."

It took a lot of wincing and maneuvering, but he managed to turn his back on me. Nick has a quick temper. It's gotten him into a lot of trouble over the years. So much trouble, in fact, that he had once been ordered to attend anger management counseling. I gave him a few moments to calm down before circling around to talk to him again. What a mistake.

"Just get out of here!" he said.

"Nick, come on . . ."

"Come on, yourself. Open your eyes, Robyn. You know when I called you yesterday and you complained you hadn't heard from me in weeks? Want to know why I didn't call sooner? It wasn't because I was busy. It was because I didn't want to. Because I'm tired of you always interfering in everyone's life. I'm tired of you being such a princess. You have it so easy. You never have to worry about anything, but you think you have the right to go around telling other people how they should lead their lives." His eyes were as hard as amethyst now. "You were right last night. I called you because I needed you. Anybody seeing you in Chinatown would figure you for some uptown shopper. No one would ever think you'd be doing anything you weren't supposed to. And you know why? Because you never do. But I don't need you now, okay? I've got it under control. Happy?

"Why don't you go back to your mommy's big house or your daddy's big apartment or go hang out with your rich-kid friends? Do whatever you want. Just get out of here and let me take care of business."

He might as well have slapped me. I felt bruised and hurt, betrayed and foolish. I told myself: *Don't cry. Don't give him the satisfaction*. But it took every scrap of strength that I had to keep the tears from dribbling down my cheeks. Nick had lied about why he wanted to see me. He had lied about what he was doing. He had lied about his job. He had probably even lied about loving me. I'd had to force the truth out of him—well, a little bit of the truth. I wished I hadn't.

My mom had warned me. She always claimed that she had nothing personal against Nick. She maintained that there was no such thing as a bad kid. "But he's not like you, Robyn," she'd said. "He's got a lot of baggage."

Maybe she was right.

He turned away from me again. I stood in the cold for a moment, staring at his back but remembering the hard look on his face. I didn't want to believe what was happening, but facts were facts. And the facts were that he hadn't called me until he needed a favor and he hadn't been honest with me about what he wanted when he did call. And as soon as he suspected that I wasn't going to help him, he'd cut out on me. If Morgan were here, she'd say, "What part of *he doesn't want you around* don't you understand?"

Well, fine. Let him do his probably illegal favor. Let him get arrested for it. Let him get put into custody again, maybe closed custody this time, with a lock on the door and a guard at the gate. It wasn't my problem. At least, that's what I told myself.

I turned and I started to push my way out of the crowd, stumbling, blinded by my tears. I kept hoping he would change his mind. Then I heard it—someone called my name.

"Robyn! Hey, Robyn!"

But it wasn't Nick's voice. It was Morgan's.

"Robyn, hey, I've been looking for you. I tried your cell, but it's off. I called Henri and she said you and Nick were here." She glanced around. "Where is he?" Then she looked at me again. "You've been crying. What happened?"

"What do you think?"

She sighed. "Nick?"

I couldn't help it. I started to cry again. Morgan rooted around in her pocket, pulled out a packet of tissues, and handed it to me.

"Did you two have another fight?"

"Something like that."

She slipped an arm around my shoulder. "Guys! They can be such a pain, right?"

Then *I* glanced around. "Where's Billy? I thought he was bringing you to the parade."

"He was—until he found out that one of the parade's sponsors is a cosmetics company—"

"That tests its stuff on animals."

"You've got it," she said. "We argued about it for a while. I always figured Billy was a pushover. But he really digs in. He absolutely refused to come. And, I don't know..." She sighed. "Billy and I are so different. Maybe it wasn't meant to be." Then her eyes got big and she said, "Hey, that looks like your sweater."

I turned in the direction she was pointing. It didn't just look like my sweater. It *was* my sweater. The handmade, robin's-egg blue sweater that my mother had brought back from England. It flashed at me from under a shabby, unzipped jacket. Whoever wore the sweater had a hat jammed down on his head, covering his forehead. He had pulled a scarf up over his mouth and the tip of his nose. And he had my backpack slung over his shoulder.

"Hey!" I shouted. "Hey, you!"

The thief's eyes met mine. At first he looked puzzled.

"That's my sweater," I yelled, pulling at the front of my jacket so that he would understand what I was saying.

His eyes widened. He froze, and for a moment I thought he was going to oblige me by standing where he was until I could grab him and pull the sweater off him. Then I realized that he was looking somewhere over my shoulder. He yelled something that I didn't understand. A second guy yelled something back in Chinese. A number of heads turned in our direction—including Nick's. I turned away from him just in time to see the guy with my backpack run away from the crowd.

"Hey!" I yelled again. "Hey, stop!"

Of course, the guy didn't stop. If anything, he pushed himself even harder. By the time I had kicked myself into gear, he had cleared the side of the hospital, cut down an alley, and was heading toward Chinatown. Well, he had picked the wrong person on the wrong day. Maybe I had been stupid. Maybe Nick had used me. But there was no way I going to let this thief make off with my stuff a second time. I kept after him. I may not be a track star, but I'm in pretty good shape. So was the thief. For a little guy, he really flew. I had to sprint to keep him in sight. After a couple of blocks, I was gasping for air. The thundering of my heart and the pounding of my feet had drowned out the dozen or so marching bands in the background and the roar of the crowd. I think that's why it took me a minute to realize that Morgan was right behind me.

"Robyn, give it up! You're never going to catch him," she said. At least, I think that's what she said. She was panting so hard that she swallowed half the words.

Then I spotted the thief speeding toward the end of a dead-end alley. He drew up short when he reached a brick wall. *A-ha*, I thought. *Trapped.* And *outnumbered*. There were two of us, and Morgan and I were both bigger than he was. I would get back my stuff for sure.

The thief turned to face us. He crouched, poised to sprint back past us. He started to bob this way and that, the way boxers do when they're trying to avoid a blow, or when they're trying to find an opening to throw their own punch. He seemed pretty confident for a small guy—at best, he came up to my shoulder, and I'm not that tall. He was slight, too, a scrawny little thing in too-big jeans. My sweater hung almost to his knees. He stared fiercely at me, ready to fight to keep what was rightfully mine.

"I don't want any trouble," I said. "I just want my stuff."

"You don't think he's armed, do you?" Morgan whispered behind me.

It had never occurred to me. I looked at the thief again. There was no weapon in his hands, and his hands were nowhere near his pockets. But that didn't mean that he wasn't carrying something lethal—a knife, maybe—and that he wouldn't use it.

"Look," I said. "Just take off my sweater and throw down my stuff and I won't call the cops."

He didn't answer. Instead, keeping his eyes firmly on me, he edged toward the building on the east side of the alley, running his hand along the rough, grimy brick as he moved. *Boomp*. His foot struck a big square of metal set into the ground next to the building. It made a hollow sound. An entrance to the sewer system? The thief stooped, still watching me, and pulled it up. He stood at the edge of the opening, slipped my backpack off his shoulder, and dangled it over the opening.

"Hey!" Morgan said, taking the word right out of my mouth.

"Don't do that," I said. But he did it anyway. He dropped my backpack through the opening. Then he jumped in after it.

Morgan and I ran to the gaping hole and stared down into it. It didn't lead into the sewers—it led into the basement of the building.

"Now what?" I said. I turned to look at Morgan, but she was looking at something else—or, rather, someone else. A big, angry-looking guy. The same guy the thief had shouted to.

"Get away from here," he said. "Get away from here now."

Morgan stood her ground.

"You don't own this alley," she said.

The guy shoved her.

"Hey!" I said. Then I saw something—a flash of color—at the mouth of the alley. The big guy must have registered my reaction, because he spun around.

Someone ran across the alley entrance. The big guy turned again to face Morgan and me.

"Move, move," he said. Only instead of trying to push us away from the entrance to the basement, he shoved us toward it. "In there, quick," he said. When we didn't move, he pushed us again, hard—first Morgan, then me. I heard a yelp of surprise from Morgan just before I fell.

CHAPTER **ELEVEN**

I put my hands out to help break my fall. It didn't help. My right shoulder took a lot of the impact and my forehead smacked the floor. As I lay there, dazed, I heard a noise overhead and something—someone?—fell on top of me. I opened my mouth to cry out, but a hand clamped itself firmly over my mouth and nose. I couldn't breathe. I panicked and started to kick frantically. I heard someone say something softly in a language I didn't understand. Then the hand slid so that it still covered my mouth but not my nose. Lips pressed up against my ears.

"Be quiet, please," a voice said. "I have a gun pointed at your friend."

Gun?

Please?

A shadow moved past me. A hand reached up and I heard a muffled metallic *clank*. Someone was locking the entrance to the basement and trying not to make too much noise doing it.

I struggled for breath and tried to find Morgan in the gloom. I was pretty sure it was the big guy holding me, which meant that it was the little guy who was locking up.

"No noise, please," the same voice said, softly. It occurred to me that he was afraid of being overheard. But afraid of whom? "If you keep quiet, we won't hurt you."

But I was already hurt. My head throbbed. Something warm and wet trickled into my right eye. *Blood,* I thought. I peered around and saw movement in the gloom. It was the smaller of the two thieves, the one who had my backpack. He came back to where we were, took the gun—it sure looked real—from the guy who was holding me, and pointed it at Morgan. For once in her life, Morgan seemed to have her sarcasm under control. The guy with the gun said something in Chinese to the guy whose hand was pressed over my mouth.

"If you cry out, they'll find us," the bigger of the two said. "If they find us, they will kill us. All of us."

They? Who were they?

My eyes were slowly getting used to the darkness, which was tempered somewhat by the light filtering through a small, grimy window set high in the wall. There was Morgan to my right. And then there were our two assailants. The first one, small and slight, was wearing my sweater and clutching the gun. My backpack was on the floor at his feet. The second one, much taller and, judging from his grip on me, much stronger, was the Chinese guy who had pushed us through the opening. The little guy whispered something to the big guy. The big guy kept his hand firmly over my mouth—there was going to be a bruise—as he jerked me away from the window.

"If you cry out, you will die," he whispered. "Do you understand?"

I nodded with an exaggerated movement so that he wouldn't mistake my answer. Slowly, carefully, he removed his hand.

"Move back there with your friend," he said. "No talking."

I went to Morgan, who was standing with her back against a brick wall. Her eyes were focused on the gun, which the little guy passed to the big guy. The little guy whispered something. That's when I caught it. I don't know why I hadn't made the connection before. The smaller one's voice was soft, almost musical, like a girl's voice. *Exactly* like a girl's voice. I took another look at him. The scarf had fallen away from his face, which I could now see was a delicate oval shape. The little guy wasn't a guy at all. She gestured to the window. From the inside, it seemed high. But from outside, it was at ground level. When I turned to look, I saw feet go by. A moment later, they were back. Four of them. Then a larger shadow fell across the window. The two of them—the girl and the guy—shrank back against the wall next to Morgan and me. The guy jammed the barrel of the gun into my ribs.

"Over here," he said.

Here was . . . a furnace, maybe, or a water heater, something big and metallic. He half-dragged me behind it. Morgan followed, pushed along by the girl. From where I was I could see one corner of the window. I hoped—okay, *prayed*—that those were police officers out there, that they'd seen what had happened, and that they were coming to the rescue. But why would the police be out there? I hadn't yelled "Stop, thief!" or "Help, police!" or anything like that. I had just shouted a lame sort of "Hey, stop!" and had taken off after the little guy, er, girl.

Something rattled. It took me a few seconds to identify the sound—someone was testing the window to see if it was locked. Then I heard a *chonk*—they were trying to lift the metal slab. It didn't give. A face appeared and pressed itself up against the window. Whoever it was cupped both hands around his face, trying to see inside. I felt warm breath on my cheek. It was the girl. Like me, she had peeked out from our hiding place. The guy tugged her back. He said something softly to her. None of us moved.

As quickly as the face had appeared, it vanished. More shadows played across the window, moving down the alley toward the dead end. A few moments later, they crossed the window again, going in the other direction. I heard voices. Whoever was out there was talking in Chinese. I had a feeling that even if I hadn't had a gun pressed into my ribs, it would not have been a good idea to call out for help. A few moments later, the voices faded and the only thing I could hear in that dark basement was the sound of the four of us breathing. Oh, and the sound of my heart, jackhammering in my chest. The guy relaxed his grip on the gun and let out a sigh of relief.

"Empty your pockets," he said.

"What?"

"Both of you, empty your pockets."

Morgan started to protest, but stopped when he turned the gun on her. We turned out our pockets. The girl scooped up our cell phones and threw them into a corner.

"Hey!" Morgan said, momentarily enraged.

The guy turned to me.

"Who are you?" he said. "Why did you chase us?"

"I chased *her*," I said, gesturing at the girl. "She's wearing my sweater."

"Robyn," Morgan hissed, turning my name into a yellow warning light. I knew what she was thinking: whoever has the gun calls the shots. In other words, be quiet. She probably thought that was the smartest thing to do under the circumstances. But I was remembering a story my father had told me.

Once, when he was still a police officer, he had responded to a call. A disturbance at a house. When he got there, the neighbors said they had heard fighting. They also told him that a young couple used to live in the house, but that now only the woman lived there. They said the couple had recently separated and the husband wasn't happy about it. They said he had always seemed so nice, so quiet. Nobody had ever seen the guy with a gun—my father had specifically asked. No one had ever heard either of the couple even mention a gun. The guy was some kind of junior accountant, they said. He didn't seem to be the gun type.

Still, my father was cautious. He said that being a cop was all about caution. He knocked at the door. After a few moments, a young woman answered. She told him that everything was fine, but he said that he could see by the look on her face that it wasn't. So he asked her if he could come into the house. Afterward, she told another officer that she had said no. My father said that he must have misunderstood. He said that he thought she had said yes, so he pushed open the door and went inside. The husband was in the front hall and, "*Of course*," my father said, "he had a gun." He told my father he shouldn't have come inside. He told him, "Now I'm going to have to shoot you as well."

The guy was upset, my father said. So he started to talk to him. At first that made the guy angry. He kept telling my father to shut up. But my dad just kept talking. He told the man that he had also just separated. He told him that he didn't want to get divorced, but what are you going to do? He told him about me and about how hard it was being a weekend dad. Pretty soon the man started talking. My father said, "Some guys, you get them talking, it doesn't make any difference, they're going to do what they're going to do. But other guys, they're basically decent people who are scared or who feel they've been backed into a corner. If you talk to those guys, if you make yourself a real person or, even better, a guy just like them, you can get somewhere."

In the end, the guy surrendered his gun. Nobody was hurt.

I looked at the two thieves. They were about my age—kids, not hardened criminals (I hoped). Sure, they had a gun. But the guy had said "please" when he wanted us to be quiet. He had begged me to understand. And, as far as I could tell, he had pushed us into this basement not because he wanted to hold us hostage, but because someone was looking for him—I was pretty sure it wasn't the police—and he didn't want us to tell whoever it was where he and the girl were. Maybe if I talked to them, if I reassured them that I wouldn't go to the police—although I wasn't sure that I wouldn't—Morgan and I could get out of this dark basement.

"I was downtown yesterday," I said. "At five o'clock in the morning. We both were." I nodded toward Morgan. "We were rescuing birds." I let that sink in. Maybe the guy was like Billy. Maybe he cared about animals. Anything was possible. "It's migration season," I said. I explained how birds are attracted by light, that they sometimes collide with office buildings. He didn't stop me, which I took to be a good sign. "That's when someone stole my backpack," I said. "With my sweater in it." I nodded to the girl. "*That* sweater."

The guy looked at the sweater. "That's *yours?*"

I nodded. "And that's my backpack."

The guy said something in Chinese to the girl. She said something in response and the next thing I knew they were arguing. At least, it sounded like an argument. The girl stood up, yanked off her thin jacket, tugged my sweater up over her head, and threw it at me.

"She says she's sorry," the guy said.

"She doesn't sound sorry," I said.

"Robyn, he's got a *gun*," Morgan said, sounding horrified.

The girl wasn't acting like she was sorry, either. She put on her jacket again and stood there in the dark, her arms wrapped tightly around her scrawny body, glaring at me. She said something else to the boy. Something angry.

"What did she say?" I said.

He hesitated. She spat more angry words at him.

"She said you must be crazy because there were dead animals in your backpack."

I'd forgotten about them. "Birds," I said.

"She said your food was stale and bad-tasting and that she wouldn't have fed it to a pig."

My food? It took a moment before I realized that she was talking about Billy's vegan snacks. There had been an assortment of them in my backpack. Which reminded me.

"Could I have my backpack, too?"

He sighed and said something else to the girl. This time she didn't argue. She picked up the backpack and chucked it at me. I unzipped the backpack and inventoried the contents. All of the DARC stuff was still there. So was my wallet. I pulled it out and thumbed through it. As far as I could tell, all of my identification was present and accounted for, but my money was missing in action. So were Billy's snacks and the dead birds. Well, I couldn't blame her for that.

"She wouldn't feed my food to a pig, huh?" I said. "Looks like she gobbled up everything I had."

"Robyn, please," Morgan said.

"We both did," the guy said. He sounded apologetic. "We were hungry."

"And my money?" I said.

"It's not what you think," he said. "We're not criminals."

I looked him directly in the eye. "I found your girlfriend wearing my sweater and carrying my backpack. All the money has vanished from my wallet. You ate all of my food. You're obviously running from someone. And you've got a gun." Okay, so maybe it wasn't smart to mention the gun. He hadn't been pointing it at me. He had relaxed as soon as whoever he was dodging had gone away and had laid the gun in his lap. But once again he wrapped his hand tightly around its grip. "Maybe you're not criminals," I said, "but you're not one hundred percent legit either."

"Robyn, *please*," Morgan said again. She was starting to sound like a tape loop.

"Look, we don't care what you're up to, do we, Morgan?" I said, standing up. The guy jumped to his feet.

Morgan stared blankly at me. I had to nudge her with my knee before she finally nodded.

"We don't care what you've been up to. As far as we're concerned, we never even saw you. We just want to get out of here, okay? My parents will worry about me if I don't get home soon. The same goes for my friend. They'll call the police." Morgan nodded vigorously on cue. "So how about it? You two can leave first. We'll wait fifteen minutes before we go. We won't even know which direction you went."

The guy seemed to be considering it. Then the girl said something. She stood up, still speaking urgently in Chinese. I looked at the guy, waiting for him to translate.

"She doesn't want you to go," he said. He was still holding the gun, but at least he wasn't pointing it at me.

"Why not? I told you, we won't go to the police. I promise."

I reached for Morgan, who still seemed dazed. I had to yank her hand hard before she understood that I wanted her to stand.

The girl clamped a hand on my arm. She was small, but she had an iron grip. When I tried to pull free, she tightened her grip. I glanced at the guy.

"Tell your girlfriend to back off," I said.

He didn't. Instead, he pressed closer to me. When he got right in my face, I saw how big he was. He forced me back a few inches at a time until my back was pressed against the wall.

"She says, what if they see you when you leave? Or what if you're lying? What if you go to the police? It's her life," he said, nodding at the girl, "so it's her decision."

"What if *who* sees us?"

The girl spoke again.

"Look, I don't know what your problem is," I said, "but it has nothing to do with us. I've got my stuff back. That's all I care about. But I'll tell you something. If you try to stop us from leaving, you're going to be sorry. Because we *will* go to the police."

He pressed closer. So did the girl. He raised the gun again. I felt the girl's breath on my cheek. My knees started to shake. I heard sniffling. Morgan. I couldn't blame her. We were in a dark basement with armed and unhappy people who obviously regarded us as some kind of threat. I still wasn't clear exactly why, except that it had to do with more than my sweater.

"Okay," I said. I tried to sound calm, but my voice was shaking. "Okay, we promise we won't call the cops. Just leave us here and take off. I don't know what's going on, but I do know that you're not going to make things any better by hurting us."

Without taking his eyes off me, the guy said something to the girl. She was shaking her head before he finished talking. I don't know what he was saying, but it must have been important to him because he didn't give up, no matter how much the girl disagreed. He kept talking. Her voice got louder. He spoke sharply to her.

She crossed her arms over her chest again, a tiny statue of defiance. He turned his attention back to me.

"I'm sorry," he said. "We have to tie you up."

"*What?*" I hadn't been expecting that. "Why?"

The girl removed her scarf and pulled something from her pocket. A knife. She started to cut the scarf into strips.

"Turn around and put your hands behind your back," the guy said to Morgan. Morgan looked at me, her eyes huge.

"Come on, you can't be serious," I said.

The girl grabbed Morgan and wrenched an arm behind her back. When Morgan tried to resist, the guy pointed the gun at her.

"Hey!" I said.

A tear rolled down Morgan's face as the girl tied her hands behind her back.

"Now you," the guy said to me.

"No."

"Robyn!" Morgan gasped.

"Please," the guy said. "I don't want to hurt you."

If I let them tie me up, we'd have no chance.

"Please," he said again. "Just do as I say and you won't get hurt. After I come back, we'll let you go."

"After you come back from where?"

"I have to go somewhere. It's important."

When I'd spotted them, he and the girl had been at the parade. Picking pockets, maybe. Or maybe looking for more unattended backpacks and sweaters.

"You're going to steal again?" I said. "You're going to go to the parade and steal from the people who are there with their kids?"

The guy stiffened. "We're not criminals."

"You steal stuff, but you're not thieves. You threaten us with a gun, but you're not criminals." Yes, my tone was sarcastic. No, I didn't care.

"Ling-Kung took your backpack"—Ling-Kung, the girl. *Took*, not stole—"because she was hungry and she hoped you had some money."

"And now you're going back to the parade to *take* some more money from other people," I said. Maybe they'd get lucky. Maybe they'd stumble across Nick with his bag full of money . . .

Oh.

I had been walking away from Nick when I spotted the girl. She had called out something to the guy, who was behind me. Behind me, not far from where Nick was standing. Nick, in his bright pink hat, carrying the bag with the Christmas tree sticker on it. A bag that held money, a visa, and a passport with a girl's photograph in it.

"She's not in this country legally, is she?" I said. "That's what this is all about, isn't it?"

Maybe underneath it all he was a nice guy, maybe he wasn't. I had no way of knowing. But one thing I did know—he would never have made it as a professional gambler. If he'd drawn four aces, you'd have known it immediately by the look on his face. Right then his expression was one of pure surprise, which told me that I had guessed correctly.

The girl, Ling-Kung, said something to him in a harsh tone. He shrugged. I looked again at her slight body and her ill-fitting clothes. I was willing to bet she hadn't been in the country very long.

"Was she smuggled in? Is that why you're hiding her? Are you working for the snakeheads?"

"The *what?*" Morgan said.

The girl stiffened. She understood the word.

"You know the snakeheads?" she said. She spoke in a soft voice in clear, but accented, English.

"I know about them," I said. "I know they smuggle people into the country. And I know nineteen people were found dead in a shipping container just a few days ago." I looked at her closely, trying to read her expression. She would have made a better gambler. "Were *you* in that container?"

She held herself as tall as she could and looked directly at me.

"She came here to join her father," the guy said. "Her brother came with her. The trip took a month, but he died when the ship was only halfway across the ocean. When her father found out, he went crazy.

"He didn't know the journey would be so terrible. When he made the journey himself a few years ago, he came as a passenger on a ship, not locked in a container. Ling-Kung said he was so crazy with grief that he didn't think about what he was doing. He got a gun and went to find the snakeheads. But they killed him."

"*Ohmygod,*" Morgan said in a hushed voice.

"The shooting in Chinatown a couple of days ago," I said.

The guy suddenly looked tired and defeated. "Ling-Kung's father."

My knees went weak. I should have let Ling-Kung keep my backpack. I should never have chased her. I didn't want to know these two.

"What about the people looking for you?" I said. "Who are they?" I don't know why I asked because I did not *want* to know the answer.

"Ling-Kung saw who killed her father," the guy said. "She followed him, tried to stop him. But they shot him. They saw Ling-Kung. They know she can identify them." I looked at her. Her face was rigid. I tried to imagine what she had been through—locked inside a shipping container with a bunch of other people. Watching nineteen of them die in the container with her, one of them her own brother. Then watching her father die right before her eyes.

"They are afraid of what she will do, who she will tell. If they find her, they will kill her."

"You mean, those guys who were after you, they're—"

"Snakeheads," he said.

"What about you?" I asked.

"What about me?"

"You don't have an accent. You must have been here a long time."

He stiffened. "I've lived here since I was two years old." He met my eyes directly. "*Legally*. I came here

154

with my father after my mother died. My father is a businessman."

"So how did you and Ling-Kung—"

"Ling-Kung's family is from Fujian. So is my father's family." He must have realized that I didn't know what he was talking about. "Fujian is a province in China. In the south. A lot of the people there are poor. A lot of them know people who have come to America, like my father. My father is a big success story. Many people there know about him. After Ling-Kung's father was killed, she didn't know what to do. She thought maybe my father would help her. She went to his office, but he wasn't there. He had left town that morning, on business. But I was there. I work for my father sometimes. At first she was afraid to talk to me. But when I explained who I was, she told me what had happened. But before I could even start thinking about what to do, I saw a car in front of the building. Some men got out. Ling-Kung recognized them—the people who killed her father. She was afraid that they were going to kill her. I hid her. The men came in. They asked for my father, but I could tell they were really looking for Ling-Kung. Finally they went away—I *thought* they went away. But they must have been watching the building. When we left to go back to my house, they saw us—chased us."

"Why didn't you just go to the police?" I said. "They would have helped her. If she told them what happened, described the people who killed her father, they would have done something about it. They would have found those men and arrested them. They would have protected her."

He shook his head. "They would also have called Immigration. They would have sent her back to Fujian."

"At least she'd be safe there."

"You don't understand," he said. "You don't know what these people are like. She wouldn't be safe there either. They would still get to her."

"Maybe she could make a deal with the police and with Immigration. If she helped them find the people who murdered her father, the people who arranged for the shipping container, maybe they'd let her stay here."

"*Maybe*," he said. He made it sound like a swear word. "*Maybe* isn't good enough. And here is not safe. She has to get away, but she can't go home. I was helping her." Helping her by going to the parade. Helping her by looking for a bright pink hat and a bookstore shopping bag. "Then you showed up and ruined everything."

"You were looking for Nick, weren't you?" I said.

The question seemed to confuse him. "Who?"

"Nick is involved in this?" Morgan said. Sounding more like her old self, she added, "I should have known."

"Did you know Mr. Li? The chef at Golden Treasures?" I said to the guy.

The girl said something in Chinese. I didn't need an interpreter to understand that my question had caught her off-guard.

"He is my uncle, my mother's older brother," the guy said. "After those men saw me with Ling-Kung, I

156

was afraid to go home—what if they were watching our house? I couldn't reach my father, so I called my uncle. He's not afraid of the snakeheads. He said he would help us."

"Help get money and papers for her, you mean?" I said.

They both eyed me suspiciously.

"How do you know this?" Ling-Kung said.

"Nick, my friend, knew Mr. Li. You were looking for someone wearing a pink hat, right?" The guy nodded slowly. "That's Nick."

Then I thought about what he had just said about Mr. Li—"He is my uncle." *Is*, not was.

"Have you been hiding out the whole time?" I said. "For the past four days?"

He nodded.

"When was the last time you talked to your uncle?"

"I haven't talked to him since the day after it happened. He told me where I should go and what to look for. Then he told me not to contact him again. He told me it could be dangerous. He said they had probably found out who I was, that they would go around to everyone who knew me. Why? What do you know about him?"

I hesitated. I didn't want to be the one to tell him, but the way this was going, it was important that he know. And there was no easy way to go about it.

"I'm sorry," I said, "your uncle died last night."

He stared at me. "Died?"

"Someone shot him," I said.

For a moment the guy stared at me in disbelief. Then he doubled over. I hoped the snakeheads weren't anywhere in the vicinity because the sound he made would have brought them running.

CHAPTER TWELVE

They talked between themselves, she in a soft lilting voice, he between gasps. He kept shaking his head. He was probably in shock. I didn't blame him. I felt a little rocky myself. This was the biggest mess I had ever been in. All I wanted to do was get out.

"Why don't you let us help you?" I said. "My father knows a lot of people. He used to be a police officer."

Ling-Kung scowled at me.

"No," she said. "No police."

"My mother is a lawyer."

"A really smart lawyer," Morgan said.

"She could help. Both of my parents could. They would know what to do."

But Ling-Kung wasn't having any of it. She kept saying, "No police. No police."

I turned to the guy with the gun. "What's your name?"

He hesitated, then shrugged, as if he felt he had nothing more to hide—or nothing more to lose. "Philip."

"Well, Philip, you've got a gun, so I guess that means you can keep us here if you want to. But then what? We can't stay here forever. Neither can you."

"I can't let you go until Ling-Kung is safe," he said.

Ling-Kung touched his arm and spoke to him softly in Chinese. Her dark eyes stared up at him, and his gazed down at her. That's when I got it. He wasn't just helping her because he'd stumbled across a poor soul who was in big trouble. Maybe that was how it had started out, but things had changed. Now he was helping her because he cared about her. Maybe even loved her.

When Ling-Kung finished what she was saying, Philip turned to me.

"You say your friend knows . . ." He paused. Pain flashed in his eyes. "Your friend *knew* my uncle."

"That's right."

"He's the person my uncle sent to help us?"

Not to help Ling-Kung. To help *us*. He was in love with her, all right.

"He has money and identity papers for her. A passport and a visa."

Ling-Kung picked something up off the floor. My cell phone. She said something softly. Philip translated: "She wants you to call your friend."

"I really think you should go to the police," I said.

Philip raised the gun and put it to Morgan's head. He looked as determined as my father would if anyone were threatening my well-being.

"Call him," he said.

"I can't. He doesn't have a cell phone. We'll have to go to the parade to find him."

He stared at me for a moment. "Okay," he said finally. "We'll go find your friend." Then he told me what I already knew. "I'll do whatever it takes to make sure she is safe. I mean it."

"What about you, Philip? How safe will you be after she's gone, if these snakeheads are as dangerous as you say they are?"

The gun wavered a little, but Philip's resolve remained firm. He said something to Ling-Kung. She opened the knife that she had used to cut her scarf into strips. She held it close to Morgan's neck. Philip said something else to her. Then he turned to me.

"You're going to help me find your friend," he said. "You and I are going to get the money. As soon as I return with the money, we will let your friend go."

The expression on Ling-Kung's face was grim and determined. "If he is not back here in one hour," she said, nodding at Philip, "I will hurt your friend. If the police come here, I will hurt your friend. If *anyone* comes, I will hurt your friend. Understand?" she said. "I have nothing. I have no life to go back to. If the men who killed my father find me, they will kill me. If I am sent back to Fujian, I will be killed. I get the money or I die. You understand?"

I understood.

I looked at Morgan. "I'll be back, I promise," I told her. "Don't worry, okay?"

"Next time Billy wants to boycott an event, I'm boycotting it too," she said. She tried to smile, but her lips were trembling. I squeezed her arm, stood up, and shouldered my backpack. Philip wanted me to bring it to carry the money and the identity papers. Under his supervision, I began to wind my way through a maze of basement rooms and corridors.

"You seem to know this place pretty well," I said.

"It belongs to my father. He owns several buildings around the city." I followed his directions until we came to a set of concrete steps with a door at the top. Philip took hold of my arm and held tightly as we climbed the steps together. Did he think I was going to make a run for it? Did he think I was going to abandon Morgan?

When we got to the top, he yanked me still and held me while he pressed an ear against the door to listen. He must have been satisfied because he opened the door a crack and peeked out. Then he nudged me through. I blinked in the brilliant afternoon sunlight.

I glanced at my watch. It had seemed as if I'd spent a lifetime in that basement, but it had only been half an hour since I'd left Nick. "He'll still be at the parade." When Nick made a promise, he kept it. When he said he was going to repay a debt, he wouldn't quit until he had repaid it in full.

"Nick probably thinks whoever was going to meet him got delayed," I said. "He'll wait."

Philip eyed me suspiciously.

"He told me that your cousin died saving his life," I said. "Your cousin who used to deliver pizza." His eyes widened in surprise, then filled with understanding. "Nick would have done anything for your uncle," I said. Including breaking a few laws. "I'm sure he'll still be there. If he isn't, I know how to contact him." Assuming, of course, that he went home after the parade and assuming that he answered his telephone when it rang.

Philip kept a grip on my arm. His eyes roved from left to right, up the alley into which we had emerged, down the alley behind us. Now that we were out in broad daylight, I took a good look at him. He looked serious. He also looked scared, and that made me nervous. But he sure didn't look like any desperado I had ever seen. He was wearing a grey knee-length wool coat over a dark gray suit, a white shirt, and a conservative tie. Everything looked grubby, probably from four days on the street, giving him the look of a disheveled junior executive. I remembered that he'd said he had been working for his father when Ling-Kung showed up.

"I was with Nick all day yesterday," I said. "He went into stores all over Chinatown. I think he was collecting money."

If Philip was surprised by this, he didn't show it.

"I don't get it," I said. "Why would all those people give him money?"

"Because they hate the snakeheads," he said. "The snakeheads lie to people about what the trip will be like.

They tell them, you'll be on a ship with good food and a swimming pool. They don't tell them they'll be locked inside a container with no way out. They don't tell them that if the authorities start to suspect the ship, the snakeheads will throw them overboard. The snakeheads don't care how many die. People here want to help, but they're afraid."

"So what happened? You and Ling-Kung ran. Then you called your uncle and he told you to lay low until he could get some money and papers for her?"

He didn't answer, but I could figure out most of it myself, based on what I had seen Nick do and what Nick had told me. People had helped the only way they knew how—they gave money.

"Where did a guy like you get a gun, Philip?"

"It's the gun Ling-Kung's father had when he went to see the snakeheads. Ling-Kung said that after he heard what had happened to her brother, he went to a countryman and borrowed a gun from him."

"A countryman? Someone he knew from back home?"

He nodded. "Someone from Fujian. Someone who helped him, the same way people are helping Ling-Kung now."

"But if her father had the gun—"

The expression on his face was bitter. "I told you. Ling-Kung followed her father. She tried to stop him. They argued. She got the gun away from him. Then the snakeheads showed up. Someone must have told them.

They believed he would make trouble for them. So they shot him. He had no weapon, but they shot him anyway."

I didn't know what to say.

We reached the end of an alley. Philip peeked out into the street. In the distance, I heard a familiar Christmas carol being blasted by a brass band. The parade wasn't over yet. Philip dragged me back toward the parade route. His eyes never stopped checking to the left, to the right, in front of us, behind us. Neither did mine, although we were probably looking for different things. He was checking that we weren't being followed or hadn't been spotted. I was looking for a cop.

We turned onto a street that ran across the parade route, just south of the hospital where I had left Nick. I wondered if he would still be there. If he was, he'd certainly hand over the bag to Philip. Then what? Would Philip really let Morgan and me go? Or would he be too afraid that we would go to the police? The crowd along the parade route hadn't thinned at all. If anything, there were even more people clogging the sidewalk. As we wove our way through the crowd, I began to search for a bright pink hat. I started by scanning the crowd where I had last seen Nick. That's when I became aware of a van driving slowly alongside us. *People trying to figure out how to get around the parade*, I thought. But where was Nick? Where was that hat? Had he given up and gone home? I started to glance at Philip, but something caught my eye.

Something pink.

Bright pink.

"Hey," I said, "there he—"

Philip yanked on the strap of my backpack. At first I didn't understand. What was he doing?

"Hey," I said again. "Over there. Look."

But he didn't. Why was he facing the street? Why was he—?

And then I saw.

The van had stopped right next to us, the rear side door partially open. I could see a man crouching inside— holding a gun. He was pointing it directly at Philip and me. He said something in Chinese and signaled for us to get inside. I looked toward the crowd, frantically searching for that flash of pink. This time I spotted it easily. Except the hat wasn't on Nick's head anymore. He was holding it in his hand; it dangled as he clung to his crutch. The bookstore bag with the big Christmas tree sticker on it hung from his other hand. He was looking directly at me and frowning, as if he knew that something was wrong but hadn't figured out exactly what.

Someone got out of the front of the van and said something to Philip. Philip tensed up—I think he was considering making a run for it. But the man grabbed his arm and said something that made Philip's face turn pale. He got into the van. Then the same man told me to get in. I stared at that gun. I turned to look at Nick. The man poked me with something hard. I don't know how I managed it—I didn't want to move and my knees were wobbling—but I obeyed. The door slid shut behind me.

The van made an abrupt U-turn and I toppled over. Then someone slapped some tape over my mouth and bound my wrists.

I felt hands moving over my body, checking my pockets. I heard the *zzzzzttt* of the zipper on my backpack being undone and felt hands rummage around inside. I glanced at the guy holding the gun. He didn't look anything like a junior executive. He looked like a serious gangster. He also looked exactly like one of the men I had seen in the alley behind Mr. Li's restaurant.

I felt cold all over, especially when I saw who else was in the van. Lying on the floor beside me, their mouths taped over, their hands trussed behind their backs, were Ling-Kung and Morgan. Morgan's eyes were wild. I could tell she had been crying. I didn't blame her.

The man with the gun signaled me to lie down. When I didn't move fast enough, he pushed me face-down onto the floor of the van. Someone threw something over me. A smelly old blanket.

.   .   .

I don't know how long we were in the van. Time can expand or collapse depending on whether you're nervous or excited or scared to death. The first time Nick had picked me up at my father's place, he had been five minutes late. It had seemed more like five hours as I paced up and down, wondering if he had changed his mind or had gotten into some kind of trouble. The evening that we spent together had lasted a couple of hours, but it had seemed more like a couple of minutes—time really does fly when you're with someone special. Maybe we were in the van for ten minutes, maybe more like thirty. All I know is that when the van finally stopped, I didn't move. I didn't dare.

The men who had grabbed us off the street spoke among themselves. Philip and Ling-Kung probably understood what they were saying, but I didn't. Then the blanket was lifted off me. Someone grabbed my arms and jerked at me to get me up. I was shoved out of the van and onto a concrete floor. I stumbled. My hands were taped behind me so I couldn't grab onto anything to steady myself. I almost fell. No one made a move to help me. My backpack slid off my shoulders and hung from my wrists. My scarf slipped off my neck. When I finally recovered my balance, I found myself face-to-face with the man from the front of the van, the one I had recognized from the alley behind Mr. Li's restaurant. This time, I barely noticed his face. My attention was one hundred percent focused on the gun in his hand.

I've seen real guns before. My father used to carry one every day. So did most of his friends. But he never let me touch it. He told me over and over: "Guns aren't toys, they're weapons. Getting shot in real life isn't like getting shot in the movies. Getting shot in real life wounds and maims and kills." The words echoed in my head.

I glanced around. We were in a huge, dark, dank building. *Some kind of warehouse*, I figured. Philip had been pushed out of the van after me, followed by Morgan and Ling-Kung. The man who had been in the back with us jumped out last. He and the man who'd been up front with the driver prodded us toward a door and down a corridor to a flight of stairs.

We were directed down the steps and along another corridor lit only by a naked lightbulb that dangled overhead. Finally, we were shoved into a small, concrete-walled, windowless room. The heavy metal door clanged shut. Then something *tchonked*. The lock.

Ling-Kung stared at the door for a moment. Then she went over to Philip and stood back-to-back with him. At first I was too rattled to pay attention to what she was doing. Then I saw that she was picking at the tape that bound Philip's wrists. She kept at it until his hands were finally free. He ripped the tape from his mouth and undid her hands. She undid mine; he undid Morgan's. I pulled the tape from my mouth, but Morgan just stood there, trembling, her arms wrapped around her body, her eyes glazed. As gently as I could, I peeled the tape from her mouth. She slid down to the floor and started to cry.

She was in shock. I think we all were. I was shaking so hard that my teeth rattled in my head.

"Those guys—" I said.

"They killed my father," Ling-Kung said.

Morgan made a gurgling sound. I didn't blame her. The men who had brought us here had already murdered someone. There had been a witness to that murder. And they had the witness. You didn't need any special insight into the criminal mind to figure out that they would want to dispose of that witness—and anyone who might be able to link them to the mess.

I sat down beside Morgan and put my arm around her. I knew I should say something, but what? "It's okay? Everything's going to be just fine?" Right.

"They didn't blindfold us," Morgan said.

True enough.

"That's bad, right?" she said.

If they had been worried that we could identify them later, they would have blindfolded us. But they didn't, which meant that they weren't worried. They knew we were never going to be in a position to identify them.

Philip said something softly to Ling-Kung. She went up close to him. He dug in his pocket and pulled out the gun. Morgan stared at it. Hope flickered in her eyes.

"They didn't take it," she said.

"They didn't even search me," he said.

"*What?*" That didn't make sense. "They searched me," I said. "They went through my backpack."

"After you left, she put our cell phones in her pocket," Morgan said, glancing at Ling-Kung. "But they took them."

Ling-Kung nodded grimly. The men hadn't taken Philip's gun. They hadn't even looked for it. They hadn't blindfolded us. They had tied us up in a way that was easy enough to get free. They had thrown us into a windowless concrete room with a thick metal door. And they had taken our phones, so that we couldn't call for help. I felt cold and dizzy and sick and numb.

They had done what they had done because they weren't ever going to let us out. They were never going to open the door. We were going to die down there.

CHAPTER **THIRTEEN**

"What happened?" I said to Morgan.

It had taken me a while to ask because Morgan had been crying. Morgan—crying! When did that ever happen? And I couldn't stop shaking. Philip was rocking back and forth the way babies do when they're upset, wishing they were in their mothers' arms. Only Ling-Kung appeared unmoved—probably, I realized, because she had been through much worse.

Finally Morgan ran out of tears. She was sitting on the floor next to me, her head resting on my shoulder. Instead of crying, she was saying, "I'm sorry." She kept repeating it. I had no idea what she was sorry about —if it hadn't been for me, she wouldn't be trapped behind a locked door.

"Morgan, what happened after Philip and I left?"

"For a few minutes, nothing," she said, "except that what's-her-name there pushed me down. I'm going to have a huge bruise on my tailbone." There was an edge of anger to her voice, which I took to be a good sign. Regular, normal Morgan tended to be outspoken. "Then all of a sudden we heard a big bang—I don't even know what it was—and she starting pulling at me to get me to stand up, but it was too late because there were three guys in the room. Three guys with guns." Her voice quavered at the memory. "They tied our hands behind our backs and took us out to the van."

"But how did they know where to find me and Philip?"

She started blubbering again. "I'm sorry," she whimpered. "I'm sorry."

"She told them," Ling-Kung said.

Morgan sobbed as if everything she cared about had just been ripped away from her. "I'm sorry, Robyn."

"They put a gun at her," Ling-Kung said, using her index finger to show me where, holding it against her right temple. "They said, tell us where the boy is or we will shoot you now."

Morgan sobbed again.

"She was scared. She said he went to the parade. With a girl. With you."

"I'm sorry," Morgan said again between sobs and great gasps for breath.

"What about Nick?" I said, suddenly afraid they would go after him. "Did you tell them about Nick?"

"I said Philip was taking you to a bank," Ling-Kung said. "To get money. No one talked about your friend."

"I didn't say a word about Nick, I swear, Robyn."

I glanced at Philip. He was leaning against the concrete wall, his head on his knees. Ling-Kung sat on the floor beside him, her arms wrapped around her knees, her face serious.

The snakeheads didn't know about Nick. That was good. It was also good that Nick had seen me get into a van. But that's where the good news ended. Nick didn't know why I had gotten into the van, or who had gotten in with me. I wasn't even sure that he cared.

Maybe, when I didn't return home, he would tell someone—assuming he cared enough to find out whether or not I had gone home. Maybe he would tell my father where he had last seen me. Maybe he would describe the van, although I doubted that he had made a note of the license plate. But would he tell my father about Mr. Li? About the money, the passport, and the visa? Would either he or my dad link the van to what Nick had been doing? Even if they did, how could they find it? It was just a nondescript gray van. For all I knew it was still upstairs, hidden safely inside the warehouse. And where was this warehouse anyway? It could be anywhere.

And how would Nick know that I had gotten into the van against my will? Maybe he thought I was with friends. On the other hand, my father knew I was spending time with Nick. When he got back, the first thing he would do is call Henri. Henri would tell him that Nick had been at her place, that I had gone to find him. I hadn't told Henri exactly where I would be. But she would assume that I had found Nick, wouldn't she? And when I didn't show up, my father would contact Nick, wouldn't he? And even if Nick didn't think there was anything wrong, my father would. He would look for me. But where would he look?

"Robyn?" Morgan said. "What are you thinking?"

"Nothing."

"You know what I'm thinking?" she said, her voice quivering with fear. "I'm thinking they're never going to open that door."

.   .   .

Morgan turned out to be wrong. About an hour after we had been locked in the room, I heard the metallic *tchonk* of the door being unlocked. When it opened, an elegantly dressed Asian man stepped into the room. Philip raised his head. His eyes widened. He sprang to his feet.

"Father!" he said.

Father?

Philip embraced the man. Only then did he step back. A question formed on his face.

"But how—" he said.

"Come, Philip," his father said, extending a hand.

"But Ling-Kung"—he gestured to her—"her father was murdered. She needs our help. And now—"

"Come, Philip," his father said again. He didn't look at Ling-Kung or so much as glance at Morgan and me. He wasn't interested in us. "I will explain everything."

"But Father, we can't leave them—"

Philip's father took him by the arm and started to guide him to the door. Philip balked.

"How did you find us?" Philip said.

"Please, son. Just come with me."

I saw the same two men from the van standing out in the corridor behind Philip's father. They were both still armed. But they weren't stopping Philip's father from taking him out of the room. Then I remembered what my father had told me, that the big snakeheads, the ones who make the most money, are often legitimate businessmen. They invest in human smuggling the way they might invest in the stock market. Philip's father was a businessman. I wondered how legitimate he was.

I glanced at Philip. He had seen the men in the corridor too. He looked from them to his father and then back to them again.

"I don't understand," he said.

The man's eyes hardened. He spoke to Philip in Chinese and pulled on his arm.

Philip wrenched himself free. He reached into his pocket and pulled out the gun. The two men in the corridor looked at it but didn't react. I dragged Morgan to the far side of the room. Philip's father signaled the men to stay where they were. Then he looked at the gun in Philip's hand and shook his head.

"Give that to me, son."

"Those men killed Ling-Kung's father," Philip said.

Philip's father stepped forward and reached for the gun in Philip's hand. Behind him, one of the armed men said something in Chinese. Philip's face went rigid. Philip's father said something, also in Chinese. He took another step toward Philip. Philip pulled the trigger.

Nothing happened.

Dumbfounded, Philip stared at the gun. He pulled the trigger again.

Nothing.

The gun wasn't loaded.

Philip's father wrenched the gun from his hand. "I'm your father," he said, "and you try to shoot me!" Stone-faced, he slapped his son. The blow sent Philip reeling. The men with the guns stepped into the room, and Philip's father spoke to them in Chinese. Then he turned back to Philip, and spoke sharply to him. He wheeled around and left the room. One of the men closed the door. I heard the lock turn.

Philip flung himself against the door, kicking at it, hammering at it, screaming his father's name, until he exhausted himself. He sank to the ground.

"What just happened?" Morgan said.

"Philip's father knew the gun wasn't loaded," I said. "How did he know that?" I looked at Ling-Kung. "Where did your father get that gun?"

"From a countryman," Ling-Kung said, her mouth twisted around the bitterness of the words she was speaking. "From someone he knew—someone who works for Philip's father."

"What did he say just before he left the room?" I said.

"He said he has to make some arrangements. That while he's doing that, I should think things over."

"Think what over?"

"What I want to do," Philip said.

"I'm sorry," Morgan said. She started to cry again. I reached for my backpack and started to root through it, looking for tissues to dry her tears. Of course there weren't any. There wasn't anything useful in my backpack.

Wait a sec, I thought. I felt around some more. I pulled something out and nudged Morgan. I opened my hand to show her what I had. She wasn't sure it would work—"What if we're too far underground?"—but she showed me what I wanted to know. Then we sat together on the floor, waiting.

An hour passed. Then another hour.

"I'm hungry," Morgan murmured.

Ling-Kung snorted. She was prowling around the room, testing the walls, testing the door and examining the ceiling. Even after we had all more or less agreed that there was no way out, she kept prowling.

More time passed. I closed my eyes and didn't open them again until I heard a noise. A *tchonk*. The door opened again. The men with the guns motioned to us to get up and face the wall. They told us to put our hands behind our backs and taped them together—mine and Morgan's and Ling-Kung's. Morgan was stone-faced now. She didn't cry. She didn't whimper. She said, "You're the best friend I ever had, Robyn."

Behind us a familiar voice said, "Philip, have you decided?"

"Yes, Father," Philip said. He stepped away from us, murmuring something in Chinese to Ling-Kung. She spat something back at him right before one of the men taped her mouth shut.

The men prodded us out into the corridor and nudged us toward the stairs. One of them led the way. The other brought up the rear, followed by Philip and his father. We started to climb. I tried not to think about where they were taking us and what they would do when we got there. I just climbed.

The man in front opened a door at the top of the stairs and went through it. I stepped out behind him, into the huge warehouse. Morgan and Ling-Kung were behind me. I looked at the van, which was parked exactly where it had been the last time I'd seen it. But my scarf wasn't lying on the ground beside it anymore. Someone must have picked it up. Not that it mattered.

"Get into the van," the man behind us said.

I started toward it. Every step I took seemed to push the van farther and farther away. This was going to be the longest walk I ever took.

From across the warehouse, someone called, "Police. Stand where you are." For a second the world went silent. Then something exploded in my ear and I dropped to the ground.

CHAPTER **FOURTEEN**

Something fell on top of me. Some*one*—Morgan. Her first instinct had also been to hit the ground. There were more explosions—gunshots, I realized. We scrambled back against the wall. I couldn't see what had happened to Ling-Kung and Philip. Morgan and I made ourselves as small as possible. Someone shouted, "Stay down, Robbie!" No one needed to tell me that. Morgan and I were already cowering on the ground.

One of the men who had brought us to the warehouse got shot. Blood sprayed everywhere before he collapsed motionless on the ground. Another man set down his weapon and raised his hands. Someone yelled at him to lie facedown on the ground and put his hands behind his head. He obeyed, moving cautiously and deliberately.

I raised my head and looked around. Philip and his father were gone. I heard footsteps, running back down the stairs. For a moment, nothing happened. Then people—cops, armed and fully armored—started to show themselves. Hands grabbed me and pulled at me and all of a sudden I couldn't breathe. My father was hugging me too hard. He released my hands and I peeled the tape from my mouth.

"Are you okay?" he said. "Are you hurt?"

I said I was fine, although I was shaking so hard that I would have fallen over if he hadn't been holding me so tightly.

Then I heard another shot—it had come from down below.

Ling-Kung started for the door to the stairs. A cop ordered her to stop.

"Philip," she said.

Half a dozen cops started down the stairs cautiously. I held my breath. Someone had removed the tape from Morgan's hands, and she was sticking close to me. Minutes passed like hours. Then someone stepped through the door—Philip. His face was pale, his eyes dazed. He looked like he was in shock. A cop said something. I didn't absorb the words. It seemed as if there were officers everywhere. Then an ambulance drove into the warehouse and two paramedics followed a cop through the door into the basement.

The man who had been shot still lay where he had fallen. The one who had surrendered was handcuffed and taken away. My father held onto me the whole time. He put one arm around Morgan and asked if she was okay. She nodded and mumbled something. I felt her trembling.

After a few more minutes, my father led Morgan and me out of the warehouse to where his car was parked.

"I want you two to stay put until I come back. Okay?"

I said okay.

"Dad, how did you know?"

"Nick called me. He said he was worried."

Nick. Thank god.

"Where is he?"

"Downtown."

He didn't mean downtown at the parade. He meant downtown with the police.

"But how did you know where we were?"

He gave me a strange look. "Didn't you activate those radio transmitters?"

"Yeah, but we didn't know if they'd work. We didn't even know if anyone would think about them because they were in my backpack when it was stolen."

"Nick saw you before you got into the van. He said he didn't know how you'd gotten hold of it, but he was positive you had your backpack with you. He remembered you telling Stan that you had transmitters in there. He figured that if they were still in there and you had a chance, you'd activate them. Turns out he was right."

.   .   .

It was nearly midnight by the time Morgan left police headquarters with her parents. Billy had come downtown with them. She had thrown herself into his arms.

They each said that the other one was right—Morgan said she shouldn't have gone to the parade. Billy said he should have gone with her. Then he kissed her, in front of her parents, in front of everyone.

My father drove Nick and me back to his place. When we got to the second floor, my father said, "Think you can make it up another flight on those crutches, Nick?"

Nick nodded. He hadn't said a word all the way home.

I sank down onto one end of my father's sofa. Nick stood awkwardly in the middle of the room, hunched over his crutches. My father went into the kitchen and opened the fridge.

"You should sit down," I said to Nick.

"I'm sorry," he said.

I patted the sofa next to me. Instead, he sat at the far end.

"I shouldn't have gotten you involved," he said.

"*You* shouldn't have gotten involved," my father said, coming into the room with two sodas and a beer. He handed us each a soda and then sank down onto an armchair and took a gulp of beer. "What were you thinking, Nick?" he said. Before Nick could answer, he held up a hand and said, "Never mind. It's probably better for both of us if you don't tell me." He took another swig of beer and then set the bottle down on the coffee table. "You're lucky that no one is pressing charges. You know that, right?"

Nick nodded. He hadn't touched his drink. I think he also knew that my father was probably the reason he hadn't been charged.

"What do you think is going to happen to Ling-Kung?" I said.

My father shrugged. "*If* she gets a good lawyer and *if* she's willing to cooperate and *if* her lawyer can make the case about what will happen to her if she gets sent back home, I think she may be able to make a deal."

"What about Philip and his father?"

Another shrug. "If Philip's father recovers, he'll be charged with everything from kidnapping to smuggling, violating immigration law, weapons charges, you name it."

"And Philip?"

"He says he was trying to stop his father from getting away and that his father's gun went off while they were struggling."

"Is he going to be charged with anything?"

"I don't know. But I doubt it. He didn't do anything except try to protect Ling-Kung." My father leaned forward in his chair. "Nick," he said, "if you ever again involve Robbie in something like this—in something even remotely like this—you're going to be in the biggest trouble you can imagine. But it won't be with the police. You understand me?"

Nick met my father's eyes. He nodded.

My father looked at him for a few moments. Then he stood up.

"I have to make a few phone calls," he said.

"It's after midnight, Dad."

He strode across the room to his office, went in and closed the door.

"I really am sorry, Robyn. After I heard what happened to Mr. Li, all I could think of was that I had to keep you out of it."

"By getting mad at me and telling me you weren't interested in me?"

"It was the only way I could think of to get you out of there. I didn't want you to get hurt."

"If you hadn't called my father, I don't know what would have happened."

"When I saw you get into that van—" His voice quavered. "I recognized one of the guys with you. He was one of those guys we ran into behind Mr. Li's place. When I saw you get into the van with him, I knew I had to do something. If anything had happened to you, Robyn, I don't know what I would have done."

I got up and went to sit next to him. It took a few moments, but finally he put his arm around me. I let him hold me for a while before I said, "Nick, the blond guy I saw, he pushed you, didn't he?"

I felt him nod. "Yeah," he said.

"Who is he?"

"Just some jerk."

"Some jerk who tried to kill you," I said.

He let out an enormous sigh. "He lives around here," he said. "He has—*had*—a dog. I used to hear it barking all the time."

So did I. Every time I approached my father's building, that dog would bark. Except for the day before the parade. That day it had been silent.

"*Had* a dog?" I said.

"I was coming home one day and I heard it yelping. When a dog yelps like that, it means something's wrong, so I decided to go take a look." I lifted my head off his shoulder so that I could see his face. "It was chained up in the backyard of this house," he said. "And this guy was hitting it with a stick and kicking it." His face was rigid. "I could tell by the way the ground was worn and by the dog sh—" He stopped. "Well, you know, I could tell that the dog spent most of its time out there, chained up. There were sores all around its neck from where it had been pulling. Anyway, I told the guy if he didn't stop, I was going to report him to the Humane Society."

"And?"

"And he told me to get lost. He told me he would report me to the cops for trespassing."

"And?"

"And I guess we got into a sort of argument over it and he called the cops."

"And Stan Rogers showed up, the cop who was here yesterday morning?"

He nodded.

"The guy got his father involved and they pressed charges. They said I attacked the guy, that it was unprovoked. I tried to tell the cops about the dog, but they didn't listen, especially after they checked me out."

That explained why Nick hadn't been happy to see Stan Rogers at my father's place. But it didn't explain everything.

"Why did he push you?"

"Because he's crazy," Nick said. "I did exactly what I told him I was going to do if he didn't start treating his dog better. I called the Humane Society. They sent someone around and they took the dog away."

"When did this happen?"

"About ten days ago."

It had been nearly two weeks since I had stayed at my father's place, which is why I hadn't noticed before that the barking dog had gone silent.

"The next thing I know, this guy is practically stalking me," Nick said. "I'd see him at the bus stop on the way to work, and he'd tell me I'd better watch out, he was going to get even with me. He must have followed me, because the next thing I know he started showing up at work with a couple of his loser friends. He told Barry that he was a friend of mine. They started to trash the place."

"Is that why you got fired?"

He nodded. "Barry told me, 'Tell your friends they're not welcome here.' Like I could do anything about it. The next time the guy and his friends came in, I tried to get them to leave. We ended up in a huge fight. So Barry fired me. The guy still didn't let up. I even saw him downtown yesterday. I don't think he followed me—I checked." That explained his behavior before we had got on the bus. "It must have been a coincidence or something."

"You mean, you saw him while you were waiting for the light to change?"

Nick shook his head. "I saw him just as we were coming out of the alley beside Mr. Li's place. I didn't want him to mess up what I had to do."

That was where he had suddenly pulled me to him and kissed me.

"So that kiss was just for camouflage," I said.

Finally, a shadow of a smile. "I ducked back into the alley with you to avoid the guy. But the kiss was real," he said.

I nestled closer to him and felt him tense up again.

"Robyn. I don't have a job. My rent's coming up. Your father's going to want to evict me."

"No he won't."

"Plus I got charged with assault because of that guy and his dog. And with my record—"

"Does your aunt know?"

He shook his head.

"Does anybody know?"

Another shake.

"Nick, you're going to have to ask someone for help."

"How can I do that? Everyone already thinks I'm a screw-up. Your dad sure seems to think so. This will just prove it."

"I don't think you're a screw-up. And neither does my dad."

"Right," he said. "I practically get you killed, and you think there's nothing wrong with me."

"Well, maybe there's room for improvement," I said. "But you were just trying to do the right thing."

He wrapped his arm around me, and we sat quietly until my father returned. When my father said we should all probably try to get to sleep, Nick said, "Can I talk to you for a few minutes, Mr. Hunter?"

. . .

The next evening, Nick was perched on a stool in my father's kitchen, slicing vegetables for a salad. I was making my world-famous chicken and mushroom casserole. We were going to surprise my father with dinner.

"So Morgan's okay?" Nick said.

"She was back to her old self at school today," I said. "But Billy won't let her out of his sight."

"What about you?"

"Me? I'm fine. You're the one with the broken ankle. Lucky for you your new job doesn't require you to walk around very much."

"It doesn't require me to walk around at all," Nick said. "At least for the first six weeks. After that, though, it's bussing tables."

My father had spoken to Fred Smith, who owned La Folie. He had hired Nick as kitchen help—mostly washing and preparing vegetables. After Nick's ankle was better, he would be a busboy. Thanks to his new job, he would be able to keep his apartment and pay the rent. My father had taken Nick down to the local police station, and they had talked to Stan Rogers about pressing charges against the guy who had pushed Nick. My father said he was pretty sure they could all reach some kind of settlement. He said he knew a lawyer—*not* my mother—who would help Nick. Nick had an appointment for later in the week.

Nick reached for a cucumber.

"Your mom gets back tonight, doesn't she?"

I nodded.

"What are you going to tell her?"

Good question.

"Don't worry," said a voice from the door. My father. "We'll think of something."

I had no doubt we would.

CHECK OUT THE NEXT BOOK IN THE
ROBYN HUNTER MYSTERIES SERIES:

OUT OF
THE COLD

"Mr. Duffy," I said, approaching him slowly. "You can't take those."

He jumped to his feet and whirled around to face me. The expression on his scarred face was hostile.

"Please," I said. It was all I had the chance to say. He looked at me, then at the stairs behind me. He rushed at me and pushed hard, throwing me off balance. I reeled backward, stumbled over, and started to fall.

#1 *Last Chance*

Robyn's scared of dogs—but she agrees to spend time at an animal shelter anyway. Robyn learns that many juvenile offenders also volunteer at the shelter—including Nick D'Angelo. Nick has a talent for troublemaking, but after his latest arrest, Robyn suspects that he might be innocent. And she sets out to prove it....

#2 *You Can Run*

Trisha Hanover has run away from home before. But this time, she hasn't come back. To make matters worse, Robyn blew up at Trisha the same morning she disappeared. Now Robyn feels responsible, and she decides to track Trisha down....

#3 *Nothing to Lose*

Robyn is excited to hang out with Nick after weeks apart. She's sure he has reformed—until she notices suspicious behavior during their trip to Chinatown. Turns out Nick's been doing favors for dangerous people. Robyn urges him to stop, but the situation might be out of her control—and Nick's....

#4 *Out of the Cold*

Robyn's friend Billy drags her into volunteering at a homeless shelter. When one of the shelter's regulars freezes to death on a harsh winter night, Robyn wonders if she could've prevented it. She sets out to find about more about the man's past, and discovers unexpected danger in the process....

LINCOLN MIDDLE SCHOOL
Learning Resource Center
District #64
Park Ridge, IL 60068

ABOUT THE AUTHOR

Norah McClintock is the author of several mystery series for teenagers, and a five-time winner of the Crime Writers of Canada's Arthur Ellis Award for Best Juvenile Crime Novel. McClintock was born and raised in Montreal, Quebec. She lives in Toronto with her husband and children.